ADVANCE PRAISE FOR *ALL I WANT IS YOU*

"Ballard cements herself as one of the genre's most binge-worthy authors. Delay those holiday plans because you will *not* be able to put this book down. Dim the lights, top off the cocoa, and snuggle up—*All I Want Is You* is the season's sweetest and steamiest addiction!"
          —Courtney Kae, author of *In the Event of Love*

"Somehow simultaneously heart-wrenching and cozy, Ballard has written the most stunning second-chance holiday romance. Filled to the brim with spice and tension, *All I Want Is You* is a fast-paced, sincere, and unputdownable read. It is a love letter to fans of the romance genre as well as those who write it. I will be revisiting Nick and Jess's love story every holiday season from here on out, just to fall in love with them all over again."
          —Hannah Bonam-Young, author of *Out on a Limb*

"*All I Want Is You* made me laugh out loud because what's not to love about this second-chance, forced-proximity, enemies-to-lovers Christmas romance about two competing authors? A fun, sexy read that romance lovers are sure to adore. Add this sugar'n'spice treat to your holiday reading list right away."
          —Holly Cassidy, author of *The Christmas Countdown*

"Falon's writing sizzles with wry humor, spiced holiday heat, and boughs of charm—this is her best yet! *All I Want Is You* is a one-sitting read that will make you believe in the miracle of happily ever after."   —Jen Comfort, author of *What Is Love?*

PRAISE FOR *RIGHT ON CUE*
One of *Elle*'s Best Romance Books of 2024

"Falon Ballard injects the Hallmark rom-com with some much-needed acidity i̶n̶ ̶t̶h̶i̶s̶ ̶H̶o̶l̶l̶y̶w̶o̶o̶d̶ ̶e̶n̶e̶m̶i̶e̶s̶ its sparkler."
          —*Elle*

PRAISE FOR *JUST MY TYPE*

"[A] charming ode to writers' passion and love."   —*PopSugar*

"Seth and Lana have instant chemistry on the page, and it's a joy to read their snarky banter that transforms into something more heartfelt. Their longing for each other, and the obstacles in their way, feel realistic. . . . A compulsively readable second-chance romance that's full of pining and laughs."   —*Kirkus Reviews*

"This entertaining rom-com from Ballard . . . refreshingly sees both protagonists undergoing therapy for their respective issues while reassessing their personal and professional goals, is one of healing and emotional growth as much as romance."
    —*Publishers Weekly*

"A clever, upbeat rom-com that will leave a smile on readers' faces and joy in their hearts. . . . A great showcase for Ballard's talents: Her voice is fresh and flirty, her characters well developed . . . and her pacing brisk and never boring. Romance readers—of all types—will be immensely entertained."   —*BookPage*

"A unique and humorous tale. Ballard hits all the right notes in a second-chance romance with smart, appealing lead characters."
    —*Booklist*

"This spicy, tropey read will have most rom-com fans declaring, 'It's just my type of book!'"   —*Library Journal*

"Falon Ballard delivers a page-turning, second-chance romance bursting with crackling banter and delightful characters, anchored by a layered, emotional, and sexy love story at the center."
    —Ava Wilder, author of *How to Fake It in Hollywood*

"*Just My Type* sparks with enemies-to-lovers wit and dazzles with Los Angeles flair."

—Emily Wibberley and Austin Siegemund-Broka,
authors of *The Roughest Draft*

"With its sharp writing, hilarious banter, and delightful characters, *Just My Type* is an absolutely perfect romantic comedy."

—Lacie Waldon, author of *The Layover*

"Everything about Falon Ballard's writing cuts straight to the heart. . . . *Just My Type* is an unputdownable showstopper!"

—Courtney Kae, author of *In the Event of Love*

"With the perfect swirl of lovable characters, sizzling chemistry, and perfectly crafted humor, Ballard's sophomore novel is a story you won't want to put down."

—Denise Williams, author of *How to Fail at Flirting*

PRAISE FOR *LEASE ON LOVE*

"[A] fun and light read . . . Ballard intersperses the book with text conversations (emojis and all) between Sadie and Jack, as well as her group conversation with her friends, that make readers feel like they're really part of the story. When Sadie and Jack's feelings for one another are finally realized, you can't help but celebrate alongside the characters." —*USA Today*

"Laugh-out-loud banter, smart characters, and heartfelt charm . . . this rom-com has it all!" —*Woman's World*

"[A] cozy romance." —*PopSugar*

"[A] quirky, heartwarming contemporary romance . . . This is a treat." —*Publishers Weekly*

"A fantastic read . . . a sharply funny roommates-to-lovers, opposites-attract rom-com." —*Booklist*

"This charming story of new beginnings and emotional growth has a sassy and likable narrator in Sadie, and the novel keeps a light tone despite touching on difficult subjects like toxic families and grief. . . . Readers who enjoy female entrepreneurs, found family, and gentle romantic leads will enjoy."

—*Library Journal*

"The romantic beats and the slow-burning attraction between [Sadie and Jack] are things to savor. . . . Ballard sweetly explores the ways they complement one another and also how they hope to reinvent themselves following catastrophic personal changes."

—*Kirkus Reviews*

"A delight on every level . . . A beautiful love story about finding something precious that seems out of reach."

—Denise Williams, author of *How to Fail at Flirting*

"A hopeful, heartwarming debut. With a relatable disaster of a protagonist and an adorably nerdy hero, this opposites-attract, roommates-to-lovers romance is a true delight."

—Rachel Lynn Solomon, author of *Business or Pleasure*
and *The Ex Talk*

"*Lease on Love* warmly and wittily underscores that none of us are perfect, but we are all worthy, we are all enough: we all deserve to be loved, not just by others, but by ourselves too."

—Sarah Hogle, author of *Twice Shy* and
You Deserve Each Other

"A crackling, compulsively readable debut about forging new career and romantic paths, finding strength in found family, and discovering what it truly means to be 'home.'"

—Suzanne Park, author of *Loathe at First Sight* and
So We Meet Again

Also by Falon Ballard

Right on Cue

Just My Type

Lease on Love

ALL I WANT IS YOU

A Novel

FALON BALLARD

G. P. Putnam's Sons
New York

PUTNAM
— EST. 1838 —

G. P. PUTNAM'S SONS
Publishers Since 1838
An imprint of Penguin Random House LLC
penguinrandomhouse.com

Library of Congress Cataloging-in-Publication Data
Names: Ballard, Falon, author.
Title: All I want is you : a novel / Falon Ballard.
Description: New York : G. P. Putnam's Sons, 2024.
Identifiers: LCCN 2024013718 (print) | LCCN 2024013719 (ebook) |
ISBN 9780593851845 (trade paperback) |
ISBN 9780593851852 (epub)
Subjects: LCGFT: Romance fiction. | Novels.
Classification: LCC PS3602.A621125 A79 2024 (print) |
LCC PS3602.A621125 (ebook) | DDC 813/.6—dc23/eng/20240328
LC record available at https://lccn.loc.gov/2024013718
LC ebook record available at https://lccn.loc.gov/2024013719

Printed in the United States of America
1st Printing

Book design by Shannon Nicole Plunkett

To Gaby Mongelli, for getting me this far

Chapter One

JESS

I used to love the holidays. All holidays, really, but Christmas in particular. I was *that* person, breaking out my decorations the day after Halloween (I love you, Thanksgiving, but not enough to stave off the garland and lights and stockings hung by the fire for any longer than absolutely necessary). You could find me ordering a grande peppermint mocha the moment the red cups were released, Mariah Carey queued up the second the clock struck midnight on November 1.

To be totally honest, I still do all of those things. My tree is already set up in the corner of my studio apartment, decked out in all her sparkly finery. Lights wrap around the metal railing enclosing my tiny balcony. And a single, solitary stocking has been hung, though not by the fireplace because I can't afford one of those. Instead, it dangles from a plastic hook right next to the tree, still hung with very much care. So yeah, I still do Christmas these days; there's just slightly less joy and fervor to my holiday rush. Now it's more like a holiday trickle. But I suppose that's normal when you get dumped on Christmas (fine, it was two weeks after Christmas, but it still counts and was remarkably shitty timing).

But this will be the year I get my Christmas groove back.

As I walk from the studio apartment the ad described as "cozy" down the five blocks to the coffee shop where I make most of my income, I try to focus on the holiday magic instead of lingering on my ghosts of Christmas past. It's been five years, but the holiday season always brings memories to the surface. So this year will be all about making new memories.

The shop is packed, and after I clock in, I barely have time to greet my favorite coworker, Josie, before I'm pulling espresso shots and foaming milk.

"Does this count as a holiday rush?" I ask her with a groan when the line has finally died down and we both have a minute to breathe.

It's the Monday after Thanksgiving, but with the crowds swarming the shop, you'd think everyone was fueling up for another run at Black Friday deals.

Josie wipes down the counter while I restock the baked goods. "All I know is that there's been a serious lack of holiday tipping." She tucks a strand of her long black hair back into her bun that's veered from sleek to messy, her golden-brown skin flushed from running around.

I suppress another groan. The owner of the coffee shop pays us well, but I was counting on some tip money this month to help tide me over until my next payment from my publisher.

People tend to be surprised when they find out I'm a

published romance author. Not because I don't seem like the type—I probably fit the stereotypical bill as far as appearances go—but because they assume authors make enough money to not have to work at coffee shops. Well, you know what they say about assumptions.

My phone vibrates in my pocket just as I'm about to head to the back for my break. My feet are already aching, and I'm only halfway done with my shift, but my mood lifts slightly when I see the email notification.

The subject line of the email from Sonia, my agent for the past seven years and also a friend, is promising. **INCREDIBLE OPPORTUNITY**, it reads. **RESPOND ASAP.**

Lately the only emails I've been getting from Sonia have been incessant questions about when she can expect my next manuscript. Hopefully this sense of urgency means something good is coming. Maybe an offer for a new IP project, or some promising news from my editor. Maybe one of my books finally earned out its advance and my next royalty payment won't be as pitiful as the last one.

I scan through the email quickly, eyes searching for something with dollar signs, some good news, something to celebrate.

It's the absolute opposite of good news. As a writer, I should maybe know a word or phrase for "opposite of good news," but spoiler alert, I spend half my writing time googling "synonym for smile," so I got nothing.

I force myself to go back to the beginning of the email and read it again. Surely Sonia is playing a very mean prank on me and is not actually suggesting what she seems to be suggesting. Because what she seems to be suggesting is fucking ludicrous, and she knows I would never, not in one million years, accept this "opportunity" she's so thrilled to present.

Jess,

I spoke with the pub team earlier today and they wanted me to pass along this invitation. As you know, the annual SVP holiday ball is coming up in just a few weeks and they would love for you to be involved in the awards ceremony! (For a second here, I thought she was going to tell me I was to be presented with an award, which would be amazing, even though as far as I know there's no money attached to any of my publisher's annual vanity awards.) **Nick Matthews is going to be receiving the Romance Author of the Year award and they want you to be the one to give it to him!** (There are so many things I would like to give Nick Matthews, and an award is nowhere on that list.) **I know you and Nick don't have the best history** (this is when I snorted out loud while reading—both times), **but I think this could be a great opportunity for some exposure. Plus, if you say no** (obviously I'm going to say no), **it makes it look like you don't want to be a team player, and you know how important it is for everyone at Saint Valentine's Press to show support for one another.** (Gag.) **WHEN you agree to do this, as I know you will because you are a smart woman who will take personal issues out of the equation and focus on the business** (sure, Sonia), **it's going to position us favorably when we pitch your next book. So think about it. Seriously. You need to say yes, Jess.** (Ugh, I can hear her voice in that tone that lets me know this "choice" is no choice at all.)

Bonus, as a presenter, SVP will cover your hotel room for the night of the ball! (Well, there is that one piece of good news because I don't think I could afford to go otherwise.) I'll wait for your official yes before I respond. Which I expect to receive shortly. Don't throw your phone at the wall—you can't afford a new one.

Warmly,
Sonia

My grip tightens around my plastic phone case—red and sparkly with a reindeer on the back, though I did forgo changing my ringtone to "Jingle Bells" this year—and I'm tempted to ignore her instructions, but Sonia is, as always, right.

I don't respond immediately to her email, like I normally would. Instead, I tuck my phone into my back pocket and vow to ignore her for at least two hours for having the audacity to even ask me to do this.

Sure, my career is not exactly flourishing. Sales for my last two books have not been what anyone would call stellar. I suppose there is a small chance that my publisher, SVP, could decide to decline my option for my next book— a book I have yet to write because writing a book requires an idea and I have exactly zero of those at the moment. But my backlist still does okay. I earned out the advance for my first contract, eventually, and even though I'm not making any bestseller lists anytime soon, I have a dedicated fan base who really loves my books.

Books that only got published because my fantastic editor, Hannah, saw something in me and in my writing. She has been with me for all five books, and the thought of not working with her anymore gives me for-real pangs in my chest. I don't want to leave her, and I don't want to leave SVP. Not just because I don't know that any other publisher will have me, but because I truly love my team.

And it's not their fault SVP publishes Nick Matthews's stupid books. Stupidly successful books that ride the coattails of the romance genre without actually being romance books themselves. The lack of a happily ever after in literally any of Nick's books hasn't stopped him from topping the *New York Times* Best Sellers list with every new release. It hasn't stopped the TikTokkers from blowing his books up, hasn't stopped Netflix from calling with their big movie money. And apparently, not writing true romance won't keep him from being named SVP's Romance Author of the Year.

Sigh.

Nick Matthews is the worst.

I hate him.

Truly, I do.

But I don't see how I can get out of this request.

Maybe I can say yes and then back out last minute due to some mysterious illness that will affect me only on the night of the holiday ball.

Somehow, I think that might be even worse than just saying no in the first place.

I pull my phone from my pocket, see that I have just enough time left on my break to call in reinforcements, and open my text thread with my two best friends, who are also romance writers, though both are with different publishers and therefore do not have to be forced into attending holiday balls and handing out awards to dicks who don't even write true romance.

ME: I got invited to present an award at SVP's annual holiday ball, but I don't know if I want to say yes or not.

ALYSSA: OMG that's amazing! That will be such good exposure!

ME: I guess. Only SVP authors and employees attend though, so it's not like it will be a whole new crowd of readers.

ALYSSA: Still, anytime you have the chance to get your name out there is good!

Alyssa writes absolutely gorgeous queer romances and tends to use a lot of exclamation points. She does it in real life too, but her positivity is so genuine it never even gets annoying.

KENNEDY: Is it just me or is it weird that your publisher hosts a holiday ball every year?

Kennedy pens epic fantasy romances, steeped in her West African heritage, and is just as fiercely loyal in real life as her fictional heroines.

We all live in opposite corners of the country—me in Brooklyn, Alyssa in Nashville, and Kennedy in LA—so the majority of our communication happens via text, with phone calls at least once a week, and an occasional Zoom if we can make our schedules and time zones work. The distance between us sucks, but it doesn't keep them from being the first people I go to when I need a virtual hug.

ME: Yes, it is super weird. Normally I'd just go for the free booze, which I will have to seriously cut back on if I'm expected to get up onstage and talk in front of people.

ALYSSA: Do you know what award you're going to be presenting? Maybe it will give you the chance to meet someone super cool! Connections are never a bad thing!

ME: Yeah. So that's the thing.

ME: The award I'd be giving out is going to Nick.

KENNEDY: Oh. Shit.

ALYSSA: Nick Matthews?

ME: No, Saint Nick. He's been writing romance novels in the offseason.

ME: Yes, Nick Matthews.

ALYSSA: Haha.

ALYSSA: Okay, so the situation isn't exactly ideal . . .

KENNEDY: Not exactly ideal? Nick Matthews is a fraud.

KENNEDY: Not to mention he broke her heart.

Yeah. So there's that. Not only is Nick Matthews the antithesis of what a romance writer should be, he was also the antithesis of what a boyfriend should be.

Nick and I met at a creative writing workshop several years ago and hit it off immediately. We were the only two there who wanted to write romance, and since the other highbrow lit-fic writers wanted nothing to do with us, we paired up to swap manuscripts. We were critique partners first, the two of us evenly matched in our skills and at the same point on our career trajectories. Our banter in real life was as fiery as that of the characters in our books, and then one night, after pizza and hashing out a third-act breakup, he kissed me.

I'd had a crush on him since the moment he set foot in the dingy multipurpose room at the local community center where our workshop met. How could I not? Not only was Nick a straight man writing romance, he was also physically perfect, in my opinion. I use the past tense because obviously I do not follow him on Instagram and have no idea what he looks like today.

Though I could probably guess that he's only gotten better-looking with time, a few strands of silver threaded through his dark hair, cut long enough so he can toss it out of his eyes, not so long as to appear unkempt. His hazel eyes are probably still just as stormy and hypnotizing, though I imagine they now occasionally peer out from behind the glasses he needs after all that time spent in front of a screen. I doubt he's lost any of his strength as he always used to work out plot holes during his time at the gym.

One thing I am sure of is that his overall hotness had basically everything to do with his success as a writer because lord knows it has nothing to do with his books.

Not that I've thought about him much in the five years since we broke up.

We were together, inseparable for three seemingly blissful years. Three years that saw us each sign with our respective agents and experience the agony of going on submission for the first time. A submission process that went very differently for each of us, even though we both ended up landing at the same imprint.

SVP was the only offer I got for my romantic comedy.

Nick's contemporary romance went to auction, where he had basically every publisher who prints romance fighting for his debut novel.

And as soon as the ink was dry on his six-figure, multi-book deal, he dumped me.

Like I meant nothing to him. Like I'd *done* nothing for him.

Despite sharing a publisher and a borough, I've managed to avoid running into him since.

But if I say yes to this presenter gig, if I do the thing I know I should to keep me on my publisher's good side, I won't be able to avoid him any longer.

ME: I don't know if I can do it. I don't know if I can stand onstage in front of our peers and say nice things about Nick Matthews and his dumb books that AREN'T EVEN ROMANCE.

KENNEDY: Can you say no?

ME: I don't think so. Sonia made it seem like she expected me to say yes. And so does the pub team.

ALYSSA: It won't be easy, I know, but you can do this, Jess. I know you can!

KENNEDY: If the choice is between saying yes or pissing off your pub team, I think you should say yes.

KENNEDY: Even though you know it kills me to give that man an ounce of credit.

ME: It might kill me too.

ALYSSA: It won't! What if I fly up to be your plus-one? I can hold your hand and make sure there's a cocktail waiting for you the moment you step offstage!

I think about drawing this out, telling her she doesn't need to do that just for little ol' me. But we both know where this is going, so why waste time?

ME: That would be amazing and I would love you forever.

ALYSSA: Yay! It's been way too long since I've seen your face anyway!

ME: Thank you for talking me off the ledge. Please be prepared for many more breakdowns over the next few weeks.

KENNEDY: That's what we're here for.

I swipe over to my email app, knowing I shouldn't delay the inevitable. The longer I put it off, the more likely I am to chicken out. So I open Sonia's email and send her a brief response: **I will do it, but I vow to hate every second.**

She responds a few minutes later with a thumbs-up emoji.

I flip off the stupid yellow phalange before making my way back to the front of the coffee shop. Luckily, the early afternoon crowd is beginning to pack up and head out. For the rest of the shop's operating hours, it will mostly be quick to-go orders, people grabbing a drink on their way to a show or a gig.

I take over for Josie at the register just in time to greet

one of my favorite customers. Hilary is witty and polite and always leaves a good tip, so basically she's a unicorn. I pour her two large black coffees, scribbling a cute holiday greeting on both cups before ringing her up.

Once Hilary is out the door, I check my phone again, but no other messages have come through. Saying yes to this presenter gig didn't magically get me a new book deal, not that I really thought it would.

"Everything okay over there?" Josie has begun cleaning up the coffee counter, getting ready to close up.

"Yeah. Just found out I have to do a writing thing I really don't want to do, but my agent tells me it's going to be good for me in the long run."

Josie snorts. "Why do agents always promise shit like that?" Josie isn't a writer, but like most baristas in Brooklyn, this is her side gig while she tries to make it in the theater world.

"To keep us from completely spiraling?"

"Too late for that, my friend. What does she want you to do?"

"Present the Romance Author of the Year award to my ex-boyfriend-slash-archnemesis." I'm not really sure if he can be my archnemesis without knowing he is my archnemesis, but Josie gets the point.

"Oof. That's rough."

"Tell me about it. Any chance Morgan won't give me the time off?" I flip the sign on the front door to Closed and begin counting out the register.

"Doubt it."

The owner of the coffee shop, Morgan, is completely supportive of our aspirational careers. She's come to all of my book launches and shares photos of my books on the shop's Instagram page all the time.

"I might have to fake some kind of life-threatening injury."

"Or"—Josie pauses her sweeping, leaning against the broom like she's about to waltz across the floor with it—"alternative plan: Show up looking incredible and let him know exactly what he's missing."

I shoot her a finger gun. "You might be on to something, my friend."

When I get back to my apartment an hour later, I open my laptop. Though instead of working on my manuscript—or even attempting to—as I should be, I spend the rest of the night searching for the perfect revenge dress.

Since I will be wearing said revenge dress to a publishing event, it totally counts as writing.

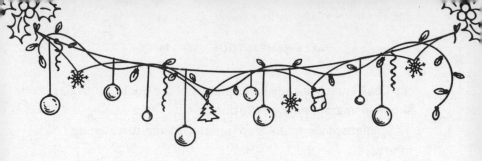

Chapter Two

NICK

One of those hideous red cups, printed with snow-flakes and confetti, with a handwritten note to have a "happiest of holidays" lands on my desk, pulling me out of my writer's-block-induced haze. I only grimace slightly, mostly because I need the caffeine and I don't care much what kind of capitalistic bullshit it's encased in, though if I had my choice, I would never see a Christmas-themed coffee cup ever again.

I fucking hate Christmas.

I push my glasses on top of my forehead, rubbing at my screen-tired eyes while inhaling at least a third of my black coffee in one long swallow.

It's only after I've set the cup down that my assistant, Hilary, sits in the chair in front of my desk, iPad at the ready. "Looks like you needed that."

"I pretty much always need that."

"I know." Hence why she delivers me fresh coffee at regularly scheduled intervals throughout the day. "How are the new pages coming?"

I groan, pinching the bridge of my nose. "They're not."

Hilary has been with me two years and knows me better than my closest friends, not that I have many of those. She handles my moods with just the right balance of indulgence and intolerance. "You'll get there. It just takes some time for the ideas to flow."

"Unfortunately, time is one thing I'm running short on." The first draft of my next book is due as soon as my editor is back from her holiday break, which means I only have about a month left.

Normally a month would be plenty of time for me to finish up a draft. If that draft had already been started. Which this one has not. The strict schedule I've kept ever since writing my first contracted book has been thrown out the window, buried in a pile of the ever-present garbage on the city's streets, and confiscated by a family of rats to use as insulation for their little rat house.

I've been staring at a blank computer screen every day, for hours a day, for the past two months, and have nothing to show for it. My eye doctor is going to kill me.

"Maybe you need to take a real break, Nick. Sitting in front of the computer all day is clearly not working for you." Hilary runs a hand through the long side of her hair, the other side buzzed in an undercut. Her pale cheeks have turned a bright pink, which means it must have been cold outside when she went on the coffee run.

Her words irritate me, even though I just thought a similar version of them myself. "This is my process, Hilary. I sit down and I write. It has worked for me for every book I've ever written."

She shrugs, her fingers stabbing at the screen of the iPad as she answers emails or responds to DMs or solves world hunger. "Well, it's not working for this one. And you do know the definition of *insanity*, right?"

I lean back in my ergonomic chair. It cost a fortune and was one of my first splurges after my advance check cleared. "So what do you suggest, I just not write for a while?" The thought is almost unfathomable. Ever since I decided I wanted to be a professional author, I have always been working on something. If I'm not editing, I'm drafting. Sometimes I'm doing both. Writing has been the one constant in my life for almost as long as I can remember. When I was a kid, it was my shield from a family I never quite fit in with, an escape. Now as an adult, my success is justification for leaving behind the family business I was supposed to join, which might account for the frenzied pace at which I write and publish my books.

Some might say I struggle with work/life balance, but for me, even though it's now become my job, writing remains that escape. It's the way I work out my frustrations and deal with my problems—by burying myself in my characters' issues instead of my own. Theirs are much easier to solve.

My therapist tells me I should work on that, which might explain why I haven't reached out to her in a while.

"I'm just saying, I think taking a break might give you the time and space to find the inspiration that you need."

"Deadlines don't wait for inspiration."

"You're Nick Matthews. Not only have you never once ever missed a deadline before, but you're SVP's highest-selling author. If you need an extension, they'll give you one." She pulls out a stylus. "Now, can we turn our attention to more pressing matters?"

"Nothing is more pressing than the writing, Hil."

"It's cute that you still think that's true after all these years in publishing, Matthews."

"Fine. Hit me." I sigh, making it long and dramatic so she knows I'm agreeing under duress.

"The SVP annual holiday ball is in three weeks." She barrels on before I have the chance to groan in protest. "You are going, as you are receiving an award. I've already booked your room at the inn." She looks up. "Do you want me to book a couple of extra nights? Built-in-vacation-slash-brain-break?"

"Sure. Why the hell not?" I cross my arms over my chest, already hating the idea.

"Great. So as I already mentioned, you'll be receiving the Romance Author of the Year award, which is the highest honor recognized by SVP."

I snort. "The highest honor they bestow upon themselves."

She ignores me, wisely. "And it looks like they've asked another SVP author to present the award to you give a little speech and go over your career highlights, that kind of thing."

That little tidbit forces me upright in my chair. Of course, there are plenty of other authors at SVP. And as far as I know, she's never once deigned to attend the holiday ball, though it's possible I might have missed her since I usually dip out after five minutes and a brief handshake with the president of the company. That fact doesn't do much to calm the waves of coffee sloshing in my stomach. I infuse a sense of calm into my voice. "Did they say who it is?"

It couldn't be her.

It won't be her.

Even if they asked her, she would never agree.

Hilary frowns, tapping some more at the screen and taking her sweet-ass time, as if the future of my mental health doesn't lie in her answer. "Someone named Jessica Carrington? Never heard of her."

My elbow knocks into my still-half-full coffee. Luckily, the puddle of brown liquid lands on the rug and not my computer. "Shit." I jump up, ready to run to the kitchen for paper towels.

But Hilary has already managed to procure a stack of napkins, soaking up the majority of the coffee before I even have the chance to move. She really is the Wonder Woman of assistants. I make a mental note to increase her holiday bonus.

Once the spill has been mopped up, we settle back into our seats. I'm hoping we can move on to the next order of business, but Hilary has other plans. "So you want to tell me why the name Jessica Carrington sent you into a full-body spasm? You guys know each other?"

I swallow, really mad at myself in this moment for the lack of coffee to drown my response in. "You could say that. We signed our deals right around the same time." Mine came a few weeks before hers, but we debuted in the same year, and had gone on submission around the same time, so it's not a total lie, though it's far from the full truth.

"And?"

Damn.

"And we used to date," I mumble.

Hilary's eyes widen. "Wait, you mean to tell me you

actually dated someone? Like a real live person? You left this apartment and everything?"

"Haha." I search my desk for something to throw at her before deciding it's probably not great to assault my employee who also happens to be my closest friend. "Is it really so hard to believe someone would want to date me?"

"No. You're a fucking catch, and you know how much I hate straight white men, so you know I really mean that." She studies me in that all-too-knowing way she has. "I'm mostly surprised you took the time away from writing to maintain a relationship."

My dating life post-Jessica can mostly be summed up with a string of short-lived nothings, probably largely to do with the reason Hilary has just mentioned. The writing comes first, always.

I shrug, though nothing about this conversation is casual. "The two were kind of linked, honestly. We were critique partners who fell in love. We wrote together, reached our first career milestones together. We did everything together for a while there." A familiar pang thunks me right in the chest. The same one I get every time I think about her. Think about how things might have been different.

Hilary softens her voice. "So what happened?"

I fucked it all up, is what happened. But I can't rehash that story right now. Or ever.

"It just didn't work out. Probably my fault." Definitely my fault.

"Well, maybe seeing her at the ball will give you guys a chance to reconnect."

I scoff. "Trust me, Jessica Carrington wants nothing less than to reconnect with me."

Hilary is smart enough to pick up on the truth behind the sentiment—that I wouldn't mind the chance to reconnect with Jess. I might have even thought about it once or twice, on the rare occasion I allow myself to search for her Instagram. She's gotten even more beautiful over the years, the warmth in her big brown eyes visible even in the tiny images on my phone screen. The joy in her smile real and genuine, like her life is that much better without me in it.

Perhaps this holiday ball will turn out to be good for something after all. Though I know there's nothing I could say to erase the past. Maybe enough time has passed that Jess would be willing to listen, hear me out.

Then again, she's one of the most stubborn people I've ever met, so probably not.

"Do you want me to request a different presenter? I'm sure SVP will follow your lead on this one."

I shake my head. "No, it's fine. If she agreed to do it, I don't want to be the one to pull out. Tell SVP I'm looking forward to the event. And book a room at the inn for the whole week after the ball."

Hilary flashes me a self-satisfied smile before heading out of my office, leaving me to stare once again at the blank screen. This time, not only can I not seem to think of anything to write, all I can seem to think about is seeing her.

"You seem extra tense today, and that's saying something. Everything going okay with the new book?" Marcus, a friend whose paycheck I don't sign, lifts the weight from my hands, setting it back on the rack before reaching out a hand to help me sit up.

On a normal day, I would lie and tell Marcus every-thing is fine, but nothing about today has been normal. So I try something new and talk about my feelings. "I found out I'm going to be seeing Jess at the SVP holiday ball. She's going to be presenting me with an award."

Marcus whistles, low and long. "Damn. No wonder you're in knots. How long has it been since you've seen her? In person, not via excessive Instagram stalking."

I throw my sweaty towel at his face, but he ducks just in time. "I haven't seen her since we broke up."

"And how long ago was that again?"

"Five years ago," I answer, though I know he knows.

"And how many women have you dated since then?"

I glare at him, moving away from the weight bench and making my way to the treadmills. I already did cardio, but I know I need to fully exhaust myself if I have any chance of sleeping tonight. "I've dated plenty of women, asshole."

"Okay, how many have you taken on more than two dates?" He jumps on the machine next to mine, bumping up his speed.

I ignore his question, ramping up my own speed to match his even though he's a much better runner than I am. He's always been a little bit more than me in all ways—taller, smarter, more charming. Looks-wise, we could be brothers, but he would be the brother everyone lusts over and I would be the brother everyone forgets about. I've known Marcus since college, and even though our lives are incredibly different—he's in charge of marketing for one of the biggest tech firms in the country and spends his free time socializing and making friends wherever he goes—we've remained friends ever since. These days our interactions are mostly limited to meetups at the gym, where I usually manage to deflect the majority of life-probing questions he throws my way.

"So I haven't met anyone I want to settle down with, big deal. May I remind you, you are also single?"

"Because I want to be, not because I'm still mooning over the one who got away. Who *you* broke up with, might I add."

I push the speed button up a couple more notches so I don't say something I shouldn't. About how much I regret that decision. And about how Marcus unknowingly played a huge role in it.

We run in silence for a few minutes before I finally bring the treadmill down to a walk, my lungs burning and my thighs aching.

Marcus slows his down too, matching my cool-down pace. "Hey, man, I'm not trying to give you a hard time."

I shoot him a look.

"Okay, I was trying to give you a hard time, but you know I'm just fucking around. I hate to see you all up in your head about this shit."

I shut the treadmill off and stand with my hands on my head, my breath slowly returning. "So any real advice for me then?"

"Yeah, man, just suck it up and apologize. Tell her how you feel."

Ha.

I listened to Marcus once and nothing worked out like I thought it would. I don't think I'll be making that same mistake twice.

Chapter Three

JESS

I spend the next couple of days waffling. I draft at least twenty emails to Sonia and my pub team, apologizing for the lack of foresight on my part, but oops, turns out I have a huge conflict on the very night of the ball and unfortunately I won't be able to be on hand to pass out a stupid unearned award to my asshole ex-boyfriend. So sorry!

I stare at those emails for hours on end, but every time I let the cursor hover over the send button, I can't seem to make myself click.

I tell myself the only reason I'm even considering showing up to this cursed event is because the fate of my career might depend on it.

I don't let myself dwell too much on the other reason. The one responsible for a little late-night Internet stalking of one Nick Matthews. The one that convinced me it was totally worth investing in the short, tight red dress that frames my tits to absolute perfection. It was a business expense, a necessary one because one quick look at his grid confirmed what I already knew—Nick Matthews has only gotten better-looking with age.

Alyssa and Kennedy tag-team checking in on me, Alyssa asking leading questions I refuse to answer, Kennedy distracting me from the impending mental spiral by talking me through the plot of my next book.

The book I should be devoting my mental energy to, instead of letting the soul-sucking Nick Matthews siphon it all away.

Speaking of soul-sucking, my phone chirps with an Instagram alert, and I jump at the chance to ignore my work in progress.

But my breath catches in my chest when I see the name on the screen.

Shit.

Maybe my stalking wasn't as subtle as I thought.

I open the app and stab at the little message icon.

@nickmatthewsauthor: Hey, Jess. Hope you're doing well. I heard you're going to be presenting the Romance Author of the Year award at the holiday ball and I just wanted to say thank you. I'm so glad you were able to put the past in the past and be there for me on this special night. It means a lot.

Wow. For someone who calls himself a writer, that sure is one boringly loaded message. Five whole sentences of complete bullshit. Be there for him? Is he fucking serious?

I click my phone off because there's no point in bothering to respond to that.

Ten seconds later, I'm punching in my passcode.

@itsjesscarrington: lol. I haven't put shit in the past, Matthews. I think your books suck. My agent told me to play nice with SVP. That's all this is.

I send the message before I can really think about it, which, I realize five seconds after the little typing dots pop up, is probably a mistake.

@nickmatthewsauthor: I understand. I won't bother you again. I just figured I would break the ice before we have to appear civil onstage in front of a room full of people who control our careers.

@itsjesscarrington: Consider the ice full-on broken. I can be professional for five minutes if you can.

@nickmatthewsauthor: I can do just about anything for longer than five minutes.

Ugh. I hate that I can hear the exact tone of voice he would use, heavy with sarcasm. We used to volley back and forth, the banter leading to laughter, and sometimes (okay, often) leading to the best sex of my life.

@itsjesscarrington: Can you though?

@nickmatthewsauthor: Hilarious. And so mature. Some things never change.

@itsjesscarrington: I know you think everything is a competition, but there's no need to try to one-up me. Don't make it more than it needs to be.

@nickmatthewsauthor: I'm not a one-upper.

I snort.

@itsjesscarrington: You are the king of one-uppers, Nick Matthews.

@itsjesscarrington: Look, I don't have time for this. I'm on deadline and I don't have the luxury of having my pub team bend to my will if I'm late. I'll see you at the stupid ball.

What I'm really late for is my shift at the coffee shop, but I'm not about to admit to him that I still have to have a day job. I throw on my coat and scarf, shoving my gloves in my pockets so I have them for the walk home later this evening.

We were graced with a smattering of snow this week, but it hasn't been thick enough to really stick and has mostly turned to a gray-tinted sludge. A white Christmas is probably not in the cards, though I'm still holding out hope. But I don't focus on the weather as I speed-walk down the streets of Park Slope. Instead, I focus on the holiday lights and garlands framing windows and draped around railings, still determined to reinvigorate my love of Christmas, even if reintroducing Nick Matthews into my life might make that impossible. I admire the trees in the front windows of the brownstones and delight in the faint notes of Christmas music spilling from businesses and cars. And I definitely don't spare even a single thought for Nick Matthews, aka the Boyfriend Who Ruined Christmas.

When I push through the door of the coffee shop, the walk has helped clear my head. Luckily, there's no line, and from the relaxed smile on Josie's face, I can assume she isn't mad at me for being a few minutes late.

I take my position at the espresso machine, leaving Josie to greet the trickle of customers throughout the afternoon.

"How is your book coming?" she asks during a particularly long lull. We've restocked the baked goods and wiped down just about every surface in the shop, so she leans her hip against the counter and levels me with a too-knowing look.

"See, the thing about writing books is I have to have an idea for the book before I can sit down to write said book." I've been stalling for so long on my option clause because I haven't been able to come up with anything that feels inspired. My mind automatically flashes back to my DMs with Nick. He never had any issue coming up with ideas, always had more of them than time to write, the lucky bastard.

And that's when it hits me. A little spark. A tiny little nugget. The seed of a book plants itself in my brain.

I freeze, not wanting to do anything to disturb the force. It's been so long since I've had this feeling, I don't want to risk messing it up, chasing away the idea before it fully forms.

"Jess?" Josie is watching me, scanning me like she's afraid I've completely lost the plot, which I literally might if I make any sudden movements.

I hold up my hand, signaling her to stop talking. I close my eyes, and yes, I know I'm being incredibly dramatic, but this drought has been long and I don't care if Josie thinks I'm rude.

I squeeze my eyes shut even tighter, and that's when I see them.

I see the characters first, two people with a history. A second-chance romance. It's the holiday season and they are forced to come together to—to what?

I open my eyes and they drift over to the flyers hung on our community notice board, catching on a bright-red one advertising a holiday musical revue.

A smile tugs on my lips. Yes. Two former lovers who have to come together to put on a holiday musical revue. Their careers depend on it being a successful show, and in order for them to do that, they'll have to overcome their old issues and learn to work together. And while they work together, they fall back in love. On the surface, it might seem a bit sweet and tame for my audience, but I know that with my voice and a few steamy scenes, I can punch it up into something holiday-tastic.

There's still work to be done, backstories to flesh out, plot points to solidify, but I can see the characters in my head, hear their voices. Their first kiss plays in my mind like I'm watching a movie in my brain.

I have it.

I don't hold back the squeal, knowing Josie will understand when I can eventually put all this into words. She doesn't resist when I grab her hands and jump around in a circle like we just won the lotto and will never have to make another latte again for the rest of our lives.

"What are we celebrating?"

I imagine at most normal jobs, if your boss caught you jumping up and down instead of accomplishing actual work, there would be some sort of retribution. But Morgan isn't that kind of boss, and the genuine smile on her face lets me know she'll be legitimately excited for me.

"I think I just got the idea I need for my next book!" I clasp my hands together, like they can hold on to the idea and keep it safe.

Josie claps for me. "I told you it would come to you eventually."

I rest my hands on my knees because that was a lot of jumping and I no longer have the lung capacity of a seven-year-old. "Not going to lie, I was getting a little freaked out."

"Congrats, Jess. I already can't wait to read it." Morgan checks her watch. "Why don't you head out early? I can stay and close up. Julie can walk Otto tonight." A queer white woman in her midforties, with a gorgeous wife, adorable dog, and impeccably decorated apartment, she's basically my inspiration for living a life on your own terms.

"Are you sure?" I'm already taking off my apron and hanging it on the hook by the back door, while I scribble some notes on receipt paper with the other hand. If she's going to give me this chance to go home and get words on the page, I'm not going to turn it down.

"Absolutely." Morgan ties on her own apron, taking my place behind the counter. "Oh, and I saw your request for time off for that holiday party. Are you sure you need just the one night?"

I grimace, the thrill of a new idea dashed by the reminder. "Yeah, I'm not going to spend any more time there than I absolutely have to."

"Sounds good. Now get home and start writing."

I wave goodbye to both Josie and Morgan, heading out into the chilly evening air with a pep in my step.

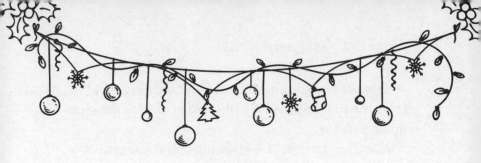

Chapter Four

NICK

My last DM to Jess goes unanswered, no matter how many times I check the thread I was idiotic enough to start. I reread our conversation more times than is probably healthy, fighting a grin the entire time. I should be disappointed by her antagonism, but I can't help but smile as I read our conversation again later that evening.

I'll take anger over indifference any day of the week.

And I forgot how fun it is to spar with her. When that verbal tension between us brought us to the bedroom after months of flirtatious banter, well, safe to say no one else has ever come close to satisfying me the way Jess did.

I scrub a hand over my face, noting the time and that I've come to the end of another unproductive writing session—minus the writing. Reaching for the top of my laptop screen, I start to close it. Surely nothing helpful is going to happen in my brain this late in the day. The only thing I've accomplished so far is pissing Jess off.

But then I freeze. My grip on the computer tightens,

but I'm too wary to move a muscle farther. I can't afford to let this sliver of an idea slide out of my head.

So I let it simmer, let it linger in the air like the phantom scent of Jess's old perfume. And then, when I'm sure it isn't going to flit away, I push the computer back open. And the words come pouring out of me.

I wrote almost four thousand words in the aftermath of my first contact with Jess in five years. Normally I'm a hardcore plotter—I plan out every single chapter with detailed summaries and descriptions before I even let myself open a new document and start drafting—but last night, I just went with it. I fell into bed well after midnight, exhausted but elated, my writer's block fully conquered.

Or so I thought.

I've been back in front of the computer for two hours this morning, and nothing has come of it. I reread everything I wrote the night before—another break in my usual process—but it hasn't done anything to jump-start my brain. That precious spark seems to have been smothered and extinguished.

Sitting back in my chair with a sigh, I curse my own stupidity. This is why I outline everything before I start writing, so when these moments of doubt strike, I already know where I should be going. Instead, I went off on some fantasy tangent and wasted whatever momentum might have come of it.

Usually when I sit down to write, I shut my phone away in a desk drawer. It's something Jess always made me do— lock away the distractions, out of sight, out of mind.

But today, she is the damn distraction. I take out my phone and open Instagram, not allowing myself to hope she might have responded to my final message.

@nickmatthewsauthor: See you then. I'll be the one receiving the award.

Okay, so it was an asshole thing to say, but she started it.

I'm about to chuck the phone back in the desk when I see the little typing bubbles pop up at the bottom of my screen. My grip on the phone tightens in anticipation.

@itsjesscarrington: The category is SVP's Most Pompous Asshole Who Claims to Write Romance but Doesn't Actually Know the Definition of the Word, right? An award that could clearly go to no one other than you!

I know she's trying to insult me, but that doesn't stop the laughter from rumbling through my chest.

@nickmatthewsauthor: Says the woman who was on the receiving end of my romantic attention for three years and never had any complaints.

@itsjesscarrington: Trust me, I had plenty of complaints.

@nickmatthewsauthor: Hmm. I seem to recall you telling me on more than one occasion that I was "the best boyfriend you ever had" and that was before the night of nine orgasms.

@itsjesscarrington: Don't you dare bring up the night of nine orgasms.

There's a pause, but I don't respond since I can see she is typing.

@itsjesscarrington: Half of them were fake.

I snicker, because I know that's not true.

@nickmatthewsauthor: You always were a terrible liar.

@itsjesscarrington: I'd rather be a terrible liar than a horrible person.

Okay, that one might actually hurt, probably because I know there's a big part of her that thinks it's true. And to be fair, the way that I ended things was horrible. I was horrible to her.

@nickmatthewsauthor: Don't you have a book to be writing? See you at the ball.

I close out of the app before she can get the last word. I can practically see her scrunched-up angry face, hear the half grunt, half scream she would utter when frustration got the best of her. It brings the smile back to my face, despite my guilt.

I turn back to my rough draft and pound out another four thousand words.

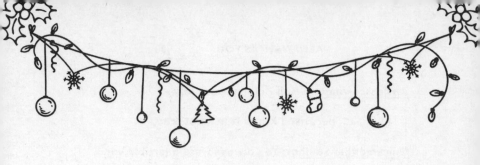

Chapter Five

JESS

The first thing I do the morning of the ball is check Instagram. It's become a ritual over the past week and a half, a sick one, but one I can't seem to break. I fully realize I am the absolute worst, but I can't help myself. I had another stellar day of writing after my last DM conversation with Nick, locking in almost eight thousand words. I also had an upsetting epiphany—the words started flowing the minute Nick Matthews slid into my DMs and started poking at me. The sparring led to a spark, and even if I don't like it, I need it, creatively.

I need to get this book done, and I need it to be good. And so I open the app and look for his response. My last message to him was cutting, maybe even slightly below the belt, but I was so sure it would lead to a fiery response from Nick, and my fingers have been itching to give it right back to him. I sent it a few days ago, hoping it would reignite this battle he himself started.

@itsjesscarrington: Of course you're running away. It's what you do best.

Except, once again, I have no new messages when I click into Instagram. I open the thread anyway, as if I haven't been fruitlessly hoping for his response—and been disappointed each time. Of course there's nothing there. Only my last message to him, with the little note of being seen.

Shit.

He saw it and he didn't respond, and so despite the stellar start I had with my manuscript, I can't help but feel like I'm right back where I started. The words were flowing better than they have in longer than I'd like to acknowledge, but once Nick stopped responding to my DMs, they dried up like an unwatered Christmas tree.

What the hell am I supposed to do now? Alyssa's flight lands in two hours and then we're leaving to head to a picturesque inn in the woods upstate. The ball is tonight. I need to get words down. And I need the safety of stoking the combative flames of this thing with Nick.

It was a life jacket, this conversation with him. It allowed me to focus on the irritation instead of wallowing in the hurt. But now he's ripped the shield away, leaving me vulnerable and exposed. The last thing I want to be in the presence of Nick Matthews is vulnerable and exposed.

I toss my phone and it lands somewhere in the rumpled sheets of my bed, where I will leave it so I'm not tempted to keep refreshing my messages. I pack my overnight bag, checking the weather outside my window every few minutes. It's been raining a ton over the past few days, but it has yet to turn to snow. I'm hoping it will hold off for just enough time to let me get to the hotel safely.

Turns out, I was hoping for the wrong thing.

Alyssa texts me an hour after I'm packed and ready to go to tell me her flight is delayed.

But delays happen all the time, especially during the holiday season and with the weather as temperamental as it is. Surely it won't take long before she's on the plane and headed my way. Because if she isn't going to be heading my way, I seriously need to rethink my plans for this whole evening. I don't think I can make it through this without her, without someone unequivocally on my side.

I don't think I can face him alone.

I try to kill some time by writing, pushing to keep up the steady pace I set for myself when I first got this new idea, but nothing is coming. I swear, it's like some magical force has invaded my brain and is keeping me from knowing where this story needs to go next.

A force named Nick Matthews.

No. I will not let him have that kind of power over me, and I will certainly not let him have that kind of power over my writing. So sparring with him inspired this second-chance romance I'm currently working on. That doesn't mean I need him to be a part of my daily life in order to finish it. I have enough memories of sparring with Nick to last a lifetime. It was our love language.

I close my eyes for a minute, harkening back to the years when Nick and I were blissfully happy. Our relationship could be baffling to those who didn't know us well, the way we lovingly insulted each other, the way we teased and chided. But it worked for us, because we were always equals. Equally talented, and on a similar career trajectory.

Until we weren't. After that, everything changed.

But I push those memories out of my head, instead

pulling up some of the good ones. The way we comple-
mented each other. The way our give and take translated
perfectly from our relationship as critique partners to our
relationship as lovers.

We clicked in bed our very first time, the tension so
deliciously taut between us that when it finally snapped, it
was explosive. But it wasn't just our off-the-charts levels
of physical chemistry that made the sex so good, it was the
way we really listened to each other. I'd never been with a
man before who obeyed when I asked him for what I
wanted. Nick seemed to take pleasure in giving me pleasure, a phenomenon I haven't experienced before or since.

Not that I haven't been with anyone else. I've dated
several people, even managed to have a sort of long-term
relationship with an investment banker named Alex. But
in the long run, we were just too different, our life philoso-
phies so unmatched, that the breakup felt like a relief.

My text alert pulls me out of a reverie I don't want to be
caught in, thinking about Nick and the good times.

ALYSSA: Bad news babe, my flight is now full-on canceled.
They're saying no flights are leaving the airport until
tomorrow evening at the earliest. I'm so sorry ☹

Shit. I guess I should have been expecting this, but I
had been holding out hope for a Christmas miracle.

ME: I totally understand. Get home safely!

ALYSSA: Are you going to be okay?

ME: I don't think I have much choice at this point. I don't
think I can just not show up.

ALYSSA: 😭 I feel terrible that I won't be there for you, but I know you can do this! Go into that ball looking like the total fucking snack you are and don't pay Nick Matthews one lick of attention!

Ha. Like I have the kind of willpower for that.

ME: I will do my best.

ALYSSA: Text us when you get there, and keep us posted on how everything is going!

ALYSSA: Love you! You got this!

ME: Love you too.

I so totally do not got this.

Chapter Six

NICK

'm glad I planned to leave for the inn early because by the time I arrive at the godforsaken spot in the middle of nowhere, the weather is looking foreboding. The rain let up slightly, but the sky is still holding those heavy clouds, the kind that might burst at any moment.

I can't help but wonder if Jess has already left the city, if she made it up here safely. If she hasn't left yet, there's a good chance she's going to get caught in the storm and miss the awards altogether. I wonder if I should message her, let her know to be wary of the weather conditions, but I can't imagine she would look too kindly on my interference.

It's too early to check into my room, so I find a comfortable corner of the lobby, near the stone fireplace, and settle in with a good book. The lobby of the inn is dressed to the holiday nines, with a large Christmas tree glittering in the middle, garlands draped over seemingly every surface, and the smell of pine and cinnamon permeating the warm and cozy room.

It makes my skin crawl.

Jess is going to love it here.

Reading has always been one of my favorite hobbies, ever since I was a little kid. My relationship with publishing has now changed my reading life in a way I never expected. It's hard for me to just sit and read and not think about my own books, or what I would have done differently if I'd written the book I'm trying to relax with. It's even harder not to drown in the imposter syndrome.

I manage to sink so deep into my reading bubble that it takes a minute before I realize someone is standing right in front of me, repeating my name. For a second, I wonder if it's her, but I would know if it were. Jess and I were so attuned to each other, I could feel the moment she walked into the room, even if I couldn't see her.

"Nick." My editor, Gina, is only a foot away from me, arms crossed and a stern look on her face. She is foreboding when she's in the best of moods, a petite Japanese American woman who is the most competent person I've ever met.

I wonder just how long she's been trying to get my attention. From the furrow on her brow, more than a minute. I hastily stick a bookmark into my novel and stand, wrapping her in a warm hug. I tower over her, but she never fails to lean into my hugs. I give good hugs. "Gina, so good to see you. Sorry, got a bit distracted."

"Must be a good book." She glances at the cover disinterestedly. "I was hoping to find you writing."

"Well, the good news is I'm making great progress." It's not a complete lie, as I did manage to get down some good words. Of course, since Jess and I stopped messaging, those words have dried up, but Gina doesn't need to know that.

"What's the bad news?"

I grin, trying to instill it with some confidence. "There's no bad news, Gina. You know me."

"Your deadline is in just a few weeks."

"And have I ever missed one before?"

She purses her bright-red lips and shakes her head. I notice then that Gina is already dressed for the big party, a shimmery black cocktail dress catching the light as she moves.

I check my watch. Shit. The whole holiday ball/awards ceremony/first in-person meeting with the former love of my life thing is supposed to start in an hour, and I still haven't checked into my room. "Gina, I would love to continue this conversation." I wouldn't, and we both know it. "But I need to get to my room and get ready." I drop a kiss on her cheek and drag my suitcase to the front desk.

An older man working behind the dark wood counter waves me over with something that could pass as a smile. "How can I help you, sir?"

"Checking in. Nick Matthews." I pull out my wallet, ready to hand over my ID.

"Nick Matthews," the man repeats.

My name is not usually misheard as it's about as basic as can be, but I spell it for him anyway.

"I'm so sorry, Mr. Matthews, but I'm not seeing your name here." The man, Stanley according to his name tag, does appear to be genuinely sorry, not that that helps much in this moment.

I close my eyes, taking in a deep breath. Luckily, my afternoon of reading has left me in a tranquil state of mind. "Could you check again? I'm here for the SVP event, and my assistant, Hilary, extended my reservation for the entire week. Hilary Jacobs? Maybe it's under her name?"

"Ah, here it is. There must have been a mix-up, but we have a Nick Jacobs, checking in today and checking out the day after Christmas?"

I let out a sigh of relief. "That must be me."

"The good news is I have your reservation. The bad news is your room isn't quite ready just yet."

I check my watch again, though I know full well we are past the designated check-in time. I don't really want to be that person, but I do have a formal event I need to be at in an hour. "Do you know when it might be ready? I was hoping to shower and change before the party tonight."

"I'm not sure, as we've had some staffing challenges today, but I promise it will be ready by the time the party is over."

Given that the holiday ball is scheduled to end at midnight, I would damn well hope so. But I know this man himself isn't responsible for the situation, so I make sure my voice is calmer than the turmoil roiling my stomach. "Is there a place I could shower and change?"

"Yes, actually. We just put in a new spa. You can get ready there, sir. My apologies for the inconvenience."

"Fantastic." I grab my bags and follow the man out of the lobby.

He leads me out into the cold, to a smaller building set in the back of the inn. He points out where the holiday party will be held, in the converted barn, and gives me a cursory tour of the property. Apparently, when the weather is good, there are all kinds of outdoor activities on the grounds.

Unfortunately, it doesn't seem like the weather is going to be good. The chill in the air is biting, and those heavy clouds seem to droop more and more each time that I look up.

I hurry into the spa building, making a mental note to see if Hilary made a reservation for a massage. My shoulders are perpetually tight from sitting in front of my computer all day, even with my fancy chair, and I could use one. The facilities here are small, but clean and warm. I don't let myself linger in the shower. My grooming routine doesn't extend much beyond combing my hair and brushing my teeth. I dress in my suit, begrudgingly tying the only tie Hilary snuck into my bag, a holiday print.

I wonder if Jess ever made it here. Somehow I don't think she checked in while I was waiting in the lobby. I would have known if she'd been in the same room with me. I'm sure of it.

Maybe she's going to bail, just not show up for this ridiculous, self-aggrandizing awards ceremony. I don't know if I would be relieved or disappointed. The pang in my chest makes me think I'd lean toward the latter, loathe though I am to admit it.

I delay walking back into the freezing cold for as long as possible, but the party started a few minutes ago, so I can't delay the inevitable any longer. I don't know what to do with my bags, but I figure I should just bring them with me, find a corner to stash them in until I've accepted my award and can get the hell out of there.

To my room, I hope.

The air stings my cheeks as I stride quickly over to the barn. The snow has finally started falling, floating down in puffy white flakes. When I step through the doors of the party, I do my best not to let out an audible groan.

I've attended this holiday ball every year since signing my contract with SVP. I know my role with my publisher, and it doesn't just include writing bestselling books. Part of my "brand" involves attending in-person events, schmoozing with my readers, and generally being a pretty face. There aren't many of us straight men out here writing romance, and sometimes my job requires me to be more of a show pony.

I'd like to say that I hate it, and sometimes I do, but I'd be lying if I said I didn't also love the thrill of validation. Think of me what you will.

This year, SVP has outdone themselves. It looks like Christmas has thrown up all over this huge old barn. The beams crossing the vaulted ceiling are wrapped in lights, as is every single post or pole or stationary object in the room. I spot three giant trees, each one decorated with enough ornaments to stock a Walmart. The tables, arranged in front of the small stage at the back of the room, are all covered in either red or green tablecloths, large floral centerpieces resting at the center of each one.

Jess is going to love it.

It's the first thought that enters my mind. Again.

I'm so fucked.

I push it out of my head and head to the check-in table. The woman sitting there takes my bags, hands me two drink tickets, and lets me know that Jessica Carrington has not checked in yet.

Yeah, I asked about that last part. Purely because I

want to see her before we're standing up on that stage to-gether. It's a business decision, really.

I can't help the niggling worry at the back of my mind that she hasn't arrived because she's stranded somewhere. What if she took a Lyft from the train station and got into some horrible accident? What if she had to abandon the vehicle and is now trudging along in the snow? What if she fell and broke her ankle and is stranded with no means of survival? Jess is not the kind of person who can last long without heating, plenty of food, and lots of cozy blankets.

My intrusive thoughts are interrupted by SVP's publicity director, who comes over to slip her arm through mine and lead me into the fray. I'm halfway grateful for the dis-traction, as I was about to charge out of the barn and march off to find Jess.

The room slowly fills with people as I'm dragged around, reintroduced to higher-ups, shaking hands and kissing ba-bies. Well, there aren't any babies at this party, but the feeling stands. No one asks more than cursory questions about my writing, instead focusing on publicity hits and movie options. It's a drag, but I know it's part of the deal so I try not to let my growing ire show.

I enviously watch some of the other writers in atten-dance as they hug one another, squealing with excitement. The romance community is vibrant and supportive and strong, but I've never really been a part of it.

My first manuscript—the one that scored me the six-figure deal I'd never allowed myself to dream of—had a happy ending when I sent it out on submission. Of course it did; all romances must. At the time, I was in a loving, committed relationship with a woman I thought I was going to spend the rest of my life with. It was easy to see my characters riding off into the metaphorical sunset because it was nothing less than what I had planned for myself.

But then I blew up my life, the love portion of it anyway. In the months that followed, the months when I was revising and editing and revising and editing, all the while questioning how I could have possibly let her get away, wondering if I'd made the biggest mistake of my life, I somehow convinced my editor that the original ending didn't really work. It was unrealistic, really, for these two people to overcome the barriers separating them. It was an ending I no longer felt I could support, and so, despite an HEA being one of the defining tenets of the romance genre, I changed it.

And since that fateful moment, none of my books have ended with a happily ever after. I always find a way for things to not work out in the end, either because of a tragedy like cancer (that one scored me my first movie deal) or because my characters make simply tragic choices. While most of the romance readers love me and my books and have accepted my stories for what they are, the other authors, not so much.

Before too long, an assistant comes to get me, leading me to the wings of the stage while the rest of the partygoers find their seats. Servers circulate through the room, pouring champagne and refilling wine. With an hour of cocktails already under their belts, the guests are loud, the chatter competing with the jazzy holiday tunes playing in the background.

"Do you know if Jessica Carrington has arrived yet?" I

ask the twentysomething woman who is guiding me up a small set of stairs and behind the curtain onstage. "She's supposed to be introducing me."

"I'm not sure. But we'll make sure she's here in time." The woman points me to a small, dark corner of the stage. "You can just wait here until you hear your cue."

No one has told me what my cue will be, or who will be delivering it, since it's easy to see Jess is nowhere to be found. I see the vice president of SVP across the stage, in the opposite wings. He gives me a smile and a cheerful wave, which I half-heartedly return.

How is it going to look to all of these execs if Jess doesn't bother to show up? She better have a good excuse for bailing.

Like being stranded in the snowy woods all by herself with no cell service.

I grimace, attempting to relax my facial muscles. I should have grabbed a drink before coming back here, but I wanted to make sure I was sharp for my big acceptance speech.

"Where the hell are you, Jess?" I mumble, checking my watch once again.

"I'm sorry, I'm sorry, I know I'm so late, I'm sorry." She arrives in a whirlwind, like she was trapped in a snow globe and only just managed to escape.

My whole body tenses, every inch of me on sudden high alert. The panicked fluster has made her voice go all breathy, and it licks up my spine.

She's here.

Jess, accompanied by another assistant, crowds into the tiny space afforded to us in the wings.

Holy fuck, she is everywhere. I lock my eyes on the other side of the stage, sure that it will only take one glance at her to send me into a total tailspin. I try to breathe through my mouth so the familiar winter jasmine scent of her doesn't overwhelm me.

She shimmies out of her coat, her elbows bumping me, the fabric skimming over my arm before she places it in the assistant's outreached hand. "Thank you so much. I apologize again for my tardiness. I'm never late, but getting here was an absolute nightmare."

My eyes are unable to stay away from her a moment longer.

She looks incredible. Beyond incredible. She's wearing a short red dress, the fabric clinging to her curves, accentuating the dip of her waist and hugging the swell of her hips. I don't allow myself to linger on the neckline, the way her breasts are practically spilling over the fabric, because I know it won't be long before I have to walk out on that stage and the last thing I need is for every one of my bosses to see just how Jess affects me.

I start listing baseball statistics in my mind, but I was never a big fan of baseball and nothing short of Santa tap-dancing across the stage with the reindeers as backup is going to let me focus on anything other than the fact that she's here, right by my side.

After a minute, she finally looks at me, hands at her side. "Nick."

It's the first thing she's said to me in five years. Just my name, uttered without a lick of emotion. And yet it sends a shiver through me that I have to work to hide.

"Jess."

The assistant steps before us, a smile on her face. "Ohmygod, Nick and Jess. How freaking cute is that? I love *New Girl*."

I purse my lips so they don't curl into a smile. We used to get that a lot. Something tells me Jess isn't exactly in the mood to reminisce about the good old days and the comparison to one of the best couples in TV history.

"Show starts in about two minutes. You guys will be on right after the VP. He'll introduce Jessica. Jessica, you'll introduce Nick. Once you're finished, you'll exit back to the wings and someone will take you to your seats."

"Thank you." I nod to the assistant, who scampers off. I wonder if she picked up on the tension, if it's as clear to everyone else as it is to me that Jess would rather be anywhere but here. I wait for her to say something, anything, but it's clear she doesn't have anything to say to me. Which is fair, I suppose. I don't know why I thought a few snarky DMs might mean she was willing to give me a chance to at least explain, but clearly I read the situation wrong.

Jessica Carrington still feels nothing for me but utter disdain.

First Christmas

JESS

"Isn't it just the most beautiful thing you've ever seen?" I stare up at the massive tree, the lights sparkling, the ginormous shiny ornaments reflecting back the scene of holiday perfection that surrounds us. When Nick doesn't immediately answer with an awed affirmative, I turn my head, excited to watch him take in the magic.

"It's . . . very big?" His gorgeous hazel eyes dart from me to the tree and back again. "Still the biggest tree I've ever seen."

"And you love it, right? You can't imagine a more perfect expression of the wonder of Christmas?" I poke at him, and even though we haven't been together long, I already know that this is our love language. I want to see how far I can push him, this little Grinch of mine.

Nick has been valiantly pretending to be as into Christmas as I am—which, to be fair, is more than most people—but the man is lacking in skills when it comes to acting.

Luckily, he is very much not lacking in other skills, which is why I'm going to let his nonexistent love for my favorite time of the year slide.

"It's very pretty," Nick concedes. He squints up at the tree again as if he might be missing something.

I wiggle my way into his embrace, resting my head on his hard chest. He's the perfect height for me, tall enough to snuggle into, not too tall that I can't reach up and plant a kiss on him whenever I want. Which I do, right at that moment. "It's okay if you don't love Christmas, you know."

"Oh thank god." His arms come around me, his chin resting on the top of my head. "I've been trying really hard, and I swear, I want to care about the holidays because I know how much they mean to you, but I just don't think I have it in me."

"Hey." I tilt my head back. "You don't have to pretend with me. I could tell from the beginning that you weren't really into all this Christmas stuff."

He glares at me. "And you let me keep up the illusion for two months?"

I grin wickedly.

Christmas season begins on November 1, and for the past almost-two months, I've dragged Nick to every holiday-themed event or location I could think of. And this is New York, so there are plenty. We've been ice-skating at Central Park, Bryant Park, and Rockefeller Center, where we currently stand, looking up at the tree. We visited Santa at Macy's and shopped for toys at FAO Schwarz and drank frozen hot chocolate at Serendipity. We saw the Rockettes and had dinner at Rolf's. We're basically living our own holiday rom-com, which is fitting, seeing as how we're romance writers.

I'd never met a straight male romance writer before, and certainly not one as gorgeous as Nick, so I assumed he was interested in more of a working relationship with me, that someone as gorgeous and talented as he is would want to keep things platonic. We became critique partners and friends, and all the while I was harboring a desperate crush on him. Which he apparently returned, given the blazing hot kiss he planted on me just a couple of months ago. We've been together ever since, and while we're definitely still early enough to be considered honeymoon stage, I can't help but hope that this honeymoon stage might last.

"Come on." I lace my fingers with his and tug him away from the crowds. "Let's go back to my place and I'll make it up to you."

"You better have something good in mind, Carrington. My knee still hurts from all the ice-skating."

I shoot him a wicked smile. "Trust me, I'll make it worth your while."

It's Christmas Eve and the tree is surrounded by people so we have to fight our way through the crowds, but Nick never once drops my hand, not until we've made it back to the apartment I share with two other girls, both of whom have, luckily, gone home for the holidays.

When Nick told me he had no plans to return to Ohio for Christmas, I encouraged my parents to take the European cruise of their dreams, leaving me to spend the alone time with Nick I crave.

As soon as the door closes behind him, I press him against it, shoving his jacket off while he wrestles with mine, our mouths coming together in the desperate, wild kisses of new love. We eventually part on a laugh, realizing it will be much easier to remove our coats if our arms aren't tangled up in each other.

Once my puffy jacket and scarf and gloves have been tossed into a heap on the floor, I work on freeing Nick from his clothes. He tugs his sweater over his head and crashes his lips down on mine, hot and demanding, his tongue sweeping into my mouth and my hands exploring the now-bare expanse of his chest and stomach.

The man is unfairly ripped for a guy who spends most of his day sitting in front of a computer.

His hands slip under the fabric of my long-sleeved T-shirt, skimming over my belly and around my back. We part for a breathless second so he can pull the shirt over my head. His eyes darken as they take in the red lace bra I wore especially for the occasion. His thumbs sweep over my nipples, already peaked and aching for his touch.

He leans down, sucking one bud into his mouth, his tongue swirling over the lace and bringing me just the barest hint of contact.

I moan, stumbling into him, our hips pressing together. He's hard, so hard, and I palm him through the denim of his jeans. He thrusts into my hand as his mouth continues to work, dampening the lace of my bra and driving me to the brink of madness.

I fumble with the button of his pants, but he doesn't stop his assault to help me. I finally get him free, my hand wrapping around the length of him before I drop to my knees.

"What are you doing?" His voice is guttural.

Instead of answering, I swipe my tongue over my bottom lip before running it up the underside of his cock.

He groans, his head falling back against the door, his hand lacing into my hair. He doesn't push or pull, but his hold tightens when I swirl my tongue around the tip, gripping tighter still when I take him in my mouth.

"Jess, holy fuck." His hips start to move, like he can't control himself, and the thought that I could bring him to this place of abandon with just a few sucks is heady.

I increase my pace. I know him well enough to know he's about to come, and I'm ready to taste him. But he pulls away before he loses it, hoisting me up and bringing me in for a kiss that knocks the wind out of me.

No one has ever kissed me like Nick Matthews. It's the kind of kiss that I've always written about, but never truly experienced until I met him.

"My turn," he growls, backing me down the hallway, his lips nipping at the sensitive spot on my neck, dancing along my collarbone.

I reach behind my back, unhooking my bra and freeing my breasts to press against his bare chest. He's got just enough hair there to tease me, my nipples still sensitive.

I fall back on the bed and Nick hovers over me, his delicious weight and warmth like the best kind of blanket. Then he removes my jeans and underwear with one swift tug, his eyes tracing over the curves of my body.

He swallows thickly. "You're so gorgeous, Jess."

I fight the urge to deflect the compliment, instead reaching for his hand, pulling him down on top of me once again, our naked limbs intertwining.

Nick's kisses turn slow and sultry, and they're somehow even hotter than the frantic ones from before. He takes his time moving down to the curve of my shoulder, the swell of my breasts. He pays such attention to them, his tongue licking and swirling until I'm writhing underneath him and I can feel the orgasm building already.

His hand skirts down the bare expanse of my belly, stroking with the lightest of touches, everywhere except for where I need him. When his fingers dance over my hip bone, I gasp, my hips rising.

He grins at me, and it's wicked. "You love this spot." He leans down to run his tongue along the crease, and the moan that escapes me is unholy.

"You know I do."

Finally, he drags a single finger up the center of me. "You're so wet, Jess. God, I can barely stand it."

I don't even have time to think before he's pushed my thighs apart and settled in between them. His tongue finds my clit as he slides two fingers inside me, and my hips buck against his face. His forearm presses down on my pelvis, keeping me at his mercy as his tongue flicks before he sucks with just the right amount of pressure. I come apart underneath him, and his mouth rides me through the wave, his strokes softening as I come down.

A minute later his mouth finds mine again, and I taste myself on his lips as he presses into me, slowly at first and then deep on one quick thrust. We just stopped using condoms a couple of weeks ago, after the all-important birth control and STI conversation, and I'm still relishing this new feeling of nothing between us.

Nick presses his forehead to mine, his breaths uneven and choppy. "How is it always so fucking good with you, Jess? I swear, it's like your body was made 'specially for mine."

My hands skate down over the muscles of his back, landing on the curves of his ass. I rock against him, meeting him thrust for thrust. "I was made for you. I love you so much."

I freeze for half a second. Make that a full ten seconds. I can't believe I just said that. We haven't exchanged the L word yet and ohmygod I just blurted it out during sex like a total idiot.

Nick freezes too, and there goes any hope that he didn't actually hear me.

I close my eyes, too embarrassed to look at him. "Shit."

But then his hand cups my cheek. "Hey. Look at me, Jess."

I open my eyes, but I don't meet his gaze until his hand slips down to my chin, grasping it gently but firmly and forcing me to make eye contact.

"I love you too." He smiles, and the light-green ring around his pupils brightens.

"You don't have to say that just because I did. I shouldn't have blurted it out like that, not when—"

"Not when I'm this deep inside of you?" He grins, shifting his hips, pressing deeper.

I can't hold back a gasp. "It's just . . . it's okay if you . . . it's early and I would understand . . ." I try to get a complete thought out, but Nick's hips continue to roll. His hand slips between us, his thumb stroking my clit, and suddenly I can't see straight, let alone form a complete sentence.

"Come for me."

I have no choice but to obey. I tighten around him as the orgasm breaks, rolling through me, wave after wave until Nick buries his face in the crook of my neck, shuddering out his own release. I hold him to me, not wanting it to end. My breaths are shaky, my skin covered in goose bumps.

"Holy shit."

He laughs, his breath tickling my neck. "That about sums it up."

I wrap my arms around his neck, threading my hands through the locks of his hair. "I've never come that hard before," I tell him honestly.

He puts enough space between us so he can look me in the eye. "Neither have I. But then again, I've never been with someone I loved before either." He tucks a lock of hair behind my ear.

"I really didn't mean to blurt that out, you know."

He presses a soft kiss on my lips. "I know. But I'm glad you did."

"Really?"

"Yeah, really. I know it hasn't been all that long, but I'm madly in love with you, Jessica Carrington."

"Madly, huh? That's a big word." I pinch his butt cheek because I'm a child.

He reaches around, grabbing my hand and lacing our fingers together. He brings our joined hands over my head, trapping me in place. "I thought I was supposed to be the one who sucked at talking about my feelings."

I know he's joking, but I also can see the hints of trepidation in his eyes. "I'm madly in love with you too."

He grins and swoops down with another searing kiss.

"Best Christmas ever?" I ask when our lips part and our eyes meet.

"Best Christmas ever," he agrees.

Chapter Seven

JESS

Leave it to Nick fucking Matthews to look like Mr. December at the exact moment I need my body to feel zero attraction toward him.

Nick doesn't wear suits often—he's a jeans and a T-shirt guy, even more casual at home. But damn if he doesn't clean up well. The man looks like he should be gracing the covers of romance novels, not writing them.

Not that any of that matters. Looks are not that important, and so what if my nipples got hard as he scanned me from head to toe? I could hear the catch in his breath as he took in my outfit, and that alone was worth the exorbitant cost of this dress that I will inevitably need to return because I can't actually afford it.

It's my first time seeing him in five years, and after the sparring in our DMs, it should come as no surprise that my body has a reaction to his.

But I'm not going to let it affect me. I'm here to do one thing, and one thing only, and that's make sure my publisher knows how dedicated I am. I'm here to secure my next book deal, and if Nick Matthews is the only way to do that, then I will suck it up.

Oof. Probably should not be thinking about sucking anything right at this moment.

Damn. Could the backstage wings of this stage be any smaller? Every time I so much as shift my weight, I brush up against him, the sleeves of his suit jacket on my bare arm causing goose bumps to explode over my skin.

If Nick notices, he doesn't say anything. He doesn't say anything at all, actually. He's probably just hoping to escape this whole situation without me completely losing my shit and blowing up at him.

I haven't ruled it out yet, but so far, cooler heads are prevailing.

Luckily, we're saved by the VP of SVP. He steps out onto the stage, leaning so close into the microphone that a screech of feedback echoes across the quieting room. He welcomes everyone to the holiday ball, expounding on the "family" that is SVP, smothering us all in the bullshit that is supposed to make up for seven-percent royalties.

He's good, though. Very convincing. I wonder how many of SVP's books he's read this year. I can almost guarantee none of mine have crossed his desk.

He's probably read all of Nick's.

And speaking of Nick, his elbow nudges me, just slightly, right in the ribs.

I turn to face him for the first time, a Medusa-level glare in place.

But he doesn't say anything, only gestures to the stage, where the VP has clearly already introduced me and is waiting for me to come take the mic.

Shit. Not exactly off to the best start, but I hurry across the stage as fast as the heels I wear maybe once a year will let me.

The VP shakes my hand before exiting the stage, and I turn to the mic and the audience. After some readings and author events over the years, I've gotten over a lot of the stage fright that used to plague me as an introvert. Tonight, it's going to be easier than usual to get through my planned speech, because I don't mean a single word of it. It'll be like acting, playing a character.

A character who thinks Nick Matthews is the best thing to happen to romance since Nora Roberts.

And so I open my mouth and the words come pouring out. Nice words, all about Nick. I don't mention how he broke my heart or ditched me as soon as he found something more important. I don't talk about how I used to have to help him write his female characters because he was as clueless as most men are to the inner workings of the female mind. I don't talk about how we used to act out his sex scenes so he could find those moments, the moments when it becomes something more than a physical joining of two bodies.

Instead, I list all his accomplishments. And there are many. I pretend like Nick Matthews has done great things for romance, when really all he's done is come in and warp it with his lack of respect for the genre.

And when I conclude my speech by announcing him as the recipient of the Romance Author of the Year award, I stand there and smile and clap, as the room gives him an ovation he doesn't deserve. Nick walks out onstage and I keep that smile frozen on my face as he takes my hand in his, pulling me close, so close that the pine and juniper scent of him fills my nose. For just a second, I allow myself to close my eyes and breathe him in, leaning into his warmth.

"Thank you." Nick brushes the words over the shell of my ear, his hand still tightly clasping mine like he doesn't want to let go.

I make myself step away, one last fake smile for the audience. I slink back into the darkened corner of the stage as Nick takes to the mic.

"I could not think of a lovelier introduction." Nick glances my way, and I wish the lights of the stage didn't wash out his hazel eyes, making them unreadable from this distance. "You might not know it, but I wouldn't be here if it weren't for Jess."

My heart jumps into my throat, lodging itself there and making itself right at home. It's the first time Nick has ever publicly noted my contributions to his career. He's never once even mentioned me in the acknowledgments section of a book, not that I've scoured every one of them looking for my name. Looking for some kind of sign that I actually meant something to him at one point in time.

"Jessica and I were critique partners for many years, and she taught me so much about writing, and characters, and love." His voice softens on that last word, and he looks my way again. "I am so thankful she was willing to be here tonight."

The crowd delivers a light, half-hearted round of applause for me.

Nick turns his attention away from the wings and focuses on the audience. Before I truly have time to process my feelings about what he said, he's walking back my way. Neither of us speaks as the same assistant leads us out to the crowd, to our table, where of course we're seated right next to each other. The spot on my left is open, having been saved for Alyssa. The spot on his right is open as well. I wonder who he was supposed to bring tonight and why she didn't show up.

I turn my attention to the glass of red wine waiting for me at my seat, downing half of it in one large gulp. Then I look around at the rest of the table and immediately realize my mistake. Nick is the guest of honor here, so of course we're seated with people whom I only recognize from their pictures on the SVP website, people I have never had so much as a Zoom call with, let alone met in person.

A couple of them shoot us inquiring looks, but then dinner is served and everyone pays more attention to their food than the midlist writer who has infiltrated their lead-title midst.

"Thank you, again, Jess. For what you said. I really appreciate you being here." Nick's words are quiet, his eyes focused on his plate.

"I didn't do it for you." I don't want him getting any ideas about why I'm really here. This is not a peace treaty or an olive branch. It's a business decision, and nothing more.

"I know," he says softly. "But I appreciate it nonetheless."

I respond with a mere *hmm*, needing this conversation to come to an end before either of us says anything bordering on emotional. I check my phone on the sly, wondering just how much face time I need to put in here before I can duck out and go check in. Since I arrived so late, I came straight to the party after a quick change in the bathroom, but if my room is anywhere near as adorable as this old barn, I'm going to enjoy holing up under the covers and snuggling with a good book. I'll take that scenario over forced human interaction literally any day of the week.

Nick is wise enough to not try to make further conversation. At least not until the dinner plates are cleared and a gorgeous Black woman slides around the table into the empty seat next to him. The two of them exchange greetings, and I don't want to eavesdrop, so I turn my attention to the other members of the table. The vacant seat next to me has created a nice barrier between me and the execs, saving me from having to fake-smile and laugh through the meal.

"Jess, I'm sure you know Lauren Reid, the executive director of publicity?" Nick leans back in his chair, allowing me to fully take in the woman next to him.

I plaster on one of those fake smiles. "No, Nick, I can't say I've ever been introduced to the executive director of publicity before." I stick out my hand. "Nice to meet you."

She gives me a firm shake and a genuine smile. "Nice to meet you as well, Jessica. I know of you, of course, but it's so nice to finally get to speak to you in person. I had no idea you and Nick had such a history." Her eyes dart between the two of us, probably picking up on the fact that we refuse to make eye contact with each other.

"We used to attend the same writers' workshop." I chance a glance at him then. The lines around Nick's mouth are tight, pulled down slightly, like he's fighting a frown at my dismissal of our relationship.

"That's so wonderful. Maybe we should have Nick be your conversation partner for your next book release. You know how much we love to see SVP authors promoting other SVP authors, and with Nick's built-in audience, it would be sure to give you a boost in attendance."

I grit my teeth. In all honesty, Lauren seems very nice, and I'm sure she's fantastic at her job, but I can think of nothing I want less than for my next book launch to be all about Nick Matthews. Assuming I even have a next book launch, as I currently have no book to launch.

But I channel my inner Sonia, seizing this opportunity as it presents itself. "Well, assuming my option gets picked up, we could maybe look into that." I smile sweetly, like I would be thrilled to have Nick deign to promote my book.

Lauren's smile fades ever so slightly. "Given your relationship with your editor, I'm sure she'll love whatever it is you're working on now."

"I hope so!" I push back my chair, reaching for the coat draped over the back. "I really hate to run, but I still need to check into my room for the night." I attempt to stick my arm through my jacket, but the stupid sleeve gets caught. "It was really nice meeting you, Lauren." I pretend like I'm not uselessly flapping the arm of the coat right in her face as I struggle to get it on.

Nick rises, calmly removing my arm from the sleeve and helping me slip easily into the coat. "I'll come with you. I actually wasn't able to check in earlier either."

"Don't leave the party on my account!" My fake laugh titters, and I hate myself a little in this moment. But what the hell is he thinking, offering to walk with me to the lobby, even if it will only take five minutes? That's five minutes too many.

"No, really, it's no trouble." Nick graciously waves to everyone seated at our table, all the high-powered people who are watching us like we're a couple of Christmas clowns. "Thank you, everyone, for the honor, and for hosting us tonight."

"Yes, thank you so much." I just manage to get the sentiment through my clenched teeth before I push through the sea of tables to the front entrance of the barn.

"Jess! Hi!" Hannah, my editor, catches me by the elbow as I'm flying by her, on a mission to get the fuck out of here.

If it were anyone else, I would keep on running, but I love Hannah, wouldn't even have a career without her, so I skid to a stop and do my best to smile. "Hannah! I wasn't sure you would be here."

She shrugs, adjusting the strap of her emerald-green knee-length dress. Hannah could have been a supermodel if she hadn't gone into publishing, tall and lithe with pale skin and waves of shiny dark hair cascading down her back. "I wasn't planning on coming, but Gina had an extra bed in her room, so I figured why not." Her dark brown eyes see right through me and my fake smile. "That was a great speech you made up there."

I grit my teeth. "Thanks. It was an honor to be asked."

She leans in close, though no one in the crowded room is paying any attention to us. The dance floor has opened, and if the "dancing" taking place is any indication, the cocktails are really kicking in. "I know how hard that must have been for you, but I promise, it will be worth it. When I take your next book to the team, even the higher-ups will know who you are now, have a face to go with the name."

I nod, not sure I can manage to make words form in my overwhelmed brain at the moment.

"Assuming you are going to have a new book to show me soon?"

I swallow the self-doubt. "Of course. I'm actually working on something right now that I think is going to be fantastic." It's only a half lie.

Her grin brightens her whole face. "Amazing! I can't wait to read it!" She squeezes my arm. "Maybe I'll see you tomorrow morning at breakfast, and you can tell me about it?"

"Sure thing." I check behind me, relieved to see Nick still tied up with the hobnobbers. I spot several other authors I've met and established relationships with over the years, people I actually want to reconnect with, but most of them are at the bar or on the dance floor, the opposite direction from where I need to be. I offer Hannah the biggest smile I can manage. "I've got to go check into my room, but I'll hopefully see you tomorrow!"

I know I will now be avoiding breakfast in the lobby, not because I don't love Hannah, but because my manuscript is nowhere near ready for her. And given how hard the writing has been over the past couple of days, I'm no longer feeling so confident in my idea.

But that's a problem for later.

After collecting my bag from the check-in table where I stashed it upon arrival, I stride through the front doors of the barn, only to be blasted in the face with freezing cold air and a flurry of white. Somewhere between me arriving at the inn and walking through these doors, the snow really started coming down. The entire acreage of the property is blanketed in white, the kind of snow that's thick, the kind of snow that sticks. I've only been inside for a couple of hours. I don't know how the skies managed to dump so much powder down in such a short period of time, but I don't pause to think about it too much.

Even my winter coat isn't enough to block out the chill, and I hunker down into it as best I can. The wind is biting, stinging my cheeks and sending snow fluttering into my eyeballs. I want to check my progress, see how much farther I have to walk before I reach the cozy warmth of the lobby, but that would require raising my head and it's not worth the cost.

I hoist my weekend bag farther on my shoulder, the weight of it combined with the wind knocking me off balance.

Then the weight of it fully disappears, and I spin around.

Nick's got my bag, resting it on top of his wheelie suitcase, though he's not having much luck with the wheels on the snow-covered path.

"I can carry my own bag!" I shout at him, fighting to be heard over the wind.

"I got it!" he yells back, gesturing for me to keep walking.

I do keep walking, because I want to get out of this weather more than I want to be right, but I don't let him know that. "It's incredibly misogynistic to imply that I'm not strong enough to carry my own bag, you know."

I don't have to look at him to know he's rolling his eyes. "I know you're perfectly capable of carrying your own bag, I'm just trying to get both of us out of the snow as fast as possible."

"I don't need you to wait for me. I know how to walk."

"Jesus Christ, Jess, I know you know how to walk. It's too damn cold to fight with you right now, so just let me do this, please."

I really hate it when Nick Matthews is right, but it really is too cold to fight. So I trudge along behind him, walking in the path made by his suitcase.

We finally make it to the lobby, and I shiver as the heat begins to seep into my bones. We pause for a minute in the entryway, and I shake the snow from my coat and my hair, letting it fall onto the black no-slip mat that's been set up for just this purpose.

"I'll take my bag back now." I hold out my hand expectantly.

Nick hands me my bag, but when I reach for it, he doesn't let go, using the movement to pull me closer. His hand reaches out, wiping a few errant snowflakes from my hair. His fingers drift down, swiping gently at my skin, clearing me of any stray bits of ice and snow.

And it has zero effect on me, the way he so carefully brushes his fingers against my cheek. And that's definitely not any sort of zing rushing through me.

"Thanks." I clear my throat, shaking my bag free from his grip and pulling it protectively to my chest. "I guess I'll see you later."

"Yeah. Later."

Later turns out to be a mere five seconds as we both

turn for the check-in desk. Both of the clerks working behind the counter look a little frazzled, a little harried, but I guess that's to be expected with the sudden onslaught of the storm during a big event.

One of them calls me over, the other gestures for Nick, so we split at the front of the line, each of us heading to opposite ends of the counter.

I offer the woman a warm smile along with my ID, letting her know right away that I don't plan to be a problem. "Jessica Carrington, checking in."

The clerk doesn't offer me much in return, but she takes my ID and taps away on her computer.

"It's really coming down out there," I comment uselessly.

She turns to me for just a second, blinking a few times in disbelief before turning back to her screen. A frown deepens on her face and a feeling of foreboding washes over me. "I'm very sorry, Ms. Carrington, but I don't seem to have a reservation under your name."

I close my eyes for just a minute, taking in a calming breath so I don't unload on this poor woman, letting her know all the reasons why I absolutely cannot handle one more problem today. "Can you check again, please? My publisher was supposed to make the reservation for me. Maybe I'm under some sort of SVP umbrella?"

The woman shakes her head. "I'm sorry, but all of the SVP-allotted rooms have been claimed."

I sigh. Of course they have. I hand over my credit card. "Can you just give me one room for tonight then? I'll check out first thing tomorrow."

I'm going to have to beg SVP to reimburse me for the

expense because this place has got to be pricy this close to the holidays, but there's no way I can even think about going back out into the snow tonight. I need a hot bath and a glass of wine, stat.

This time the woman looks genuinely upset. "Unfortunately, all of our rooms are booked. We don't have a room to sell you, I'm afraid."

I'd like to tell you that this simple bit of information doesn't bring a tear to my eye, but that would be a lie. This day has been a total disaster, from Alyssa's flight cancellation, to running late for the party, to having to sit next to Nick at dinner, and now it looks like I have no choice but to go back into the ever-worsening storm.

"Fine. Could you call me a cab to the train station then?" I start buttoning up my coat, rooting around in my bag for my hat, scarf, and gloves.

"The trains aren't running, and I don't think you'll be able to get a cab either." She looks at me with so much pity it clears the tears from my eyes. "You're welcome to stay here in the lobby. I know it isn't much, but at least you'll be out of the cold."

"That won't be necessary." Nick bends down, once again taking my bag in his hands. "I have a room. You can stay with me."

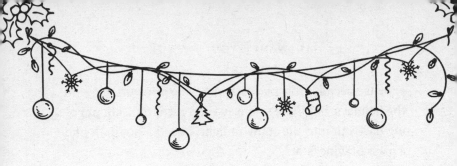

Chapter Eight

NICK

know I shouldn't have been eavesdropping on Jess's conversation at the check-in desk, but honestly, I'm glad I did. Like I'm going to let her sleep in the lobby of a hotel when I have a perfectly good room upstairs.

"Absolutely not." Like she is going to let this be an easy decision. "There is no way in hell I'm sharing a room with you."

I hoist her bag over my shoulder and grab my suitcase with the other hand. "Jessica, for once in your life can you not argue with me and just go with it?" I turn toward the elevator, marching across the lobby, knowing she'll follow me since I have all of her stuff.

"Geez, Nick, not even your heroes are as bullheaded and stubborn as you are, and they're supposed to be misogynistic."

I stop in my tracks, spinning around to face her. "Excuse me, but neither I nor my heroes are misogynistic. We're strong yet sensitive men. I'm just trying to keep you from having to sleep in the hotel lobby."

"What you're doing is railroading me and not giving me

a say in what happens in my own fucking life!" She seems surprised by the force of her words, her eyes widening as they land.

But they have their desired effect, cutting deeper than she probably intended, more layers of truth under them than she even knows. I drop a mask over my face so she can't see how much her words hurt. "You're right. I'm sorry." I hand her back her bag. "I have a room reserved here for the rest of the week. You are more than welcome to crash there for as long as needed. But you are a strong, independent woman and you certainly don't need me to make decisions for you." The words tickle at the back of my throat, like the ghost of our past has somehow lodged itself there. "Have a good night."

I barely make it ten feet.

"Wait." Her sigh is long-suffering, and since I still have my back turned to her, I let myself smile, just a little.

I pause, allowing her to catch up with me.

"This doesn't mean anything. I will only be staying in your room for one night. And only because I need a hot bath, like, yesterday."

"Noted." I call the elevator and hold the door while she steps inside first, trying not to think too hard about Jess in the bathtub, and push the button for the top level.

"Of course they put you up in some kind of penthouse suite," she grumbles, under her breath but not really.

"Pretty sure this place doesn't have a penthouse."

When the doors open, we step out and I lead the way down the hallway. As soon as I open the door to the room, it's clear I was right about the lack of a penthouse. The room can only be called cozy, with a large king-sized bed taking up most of the space. There's a dresser with a small TV resting on top, and a single armchair next to what looks to be an old-fashioned wood-burning stove. The stove seems to be purely ornamental as there is no heat stemming from it and no wood anywhere to be found. There is, however, a whole lot of plaid. On just about every available surface.

Jess immediately veers toward the bathroom and comes out with something close to a smile on her face. "There's a tub."

Bathtubs used to be her one hotel requirement when we went on vacation, since neither of our Brooklyn apartments were big enough for one. I imagine she'll linger in there for hours. The thought stokes a memory, of Jess naked and slick with water, straddling me in the tub, rocking over me gently, driving me to the edge and back so many times I finally hoisted her out of the water and bent her over the bathroom counter, stroking into her until we both screamed.

Jess tosses her bag into the armchair and it lands with a thud, forcing my mind to stop the replay just in time. My dick is half-hard, and I hastily move my hand to cover it. Luckily, she seems to be looking everywhere but at me.

I clear my throat. "If it's okay with you, I'll take a quick shower before you get in the bath. That way you can take as long as you want." At least if she spends an hour in the bath, it's one more hour we don't have to try to force conversation.

She nods, unzipping her bag and rifling through, apparently looking for nothing since she comes up empty-handed. "Sounds good."

I open my own bag, pulling out a pair of pajama pants, a plain white tee, and a clean pair of boxers before putting some much-needed separation between us in the form of the bathroom door.

Stripping out of my suit in the privacy of the bathroom feels like the best kind of relief. I hate dressing up, and everything about this evening has made the suit feel suffocating. The water pressure in the shower is surprisingly strong and I let it wash over me, easing the tension in my muscles. I feel like I've been clenched tight ever since stepping foot into the party, but the steam and the heat help ease the strain.

For a half second I consider jacking off, just to get it out of my system before my brain can play any further tricks on me. Before I have to consider sharing that bed with her. But something about it feels wrong, so despite the peace I find under the water stream, I step out of the shower after just a few minutes. I dress quickly, then open the door to the bathroom, letting out a cloud of steam.

"All yours." I hang up my suit in the closet so I don't have to watch her slip into the bathroom and shut the door between us.

Pulling my book from my bag, I turn down the sheets of the bed and make myself comfortable on the right-hand side. Jess always preferred the left, and even after all these years, I still gravitate toward "my" side of the bed. Normally, I don't listen to music while I read, but I don't want to overhear a smidge of what's happening on the other side of this wall, so I slip in some earbuds and push Play on my relax playlist.

I'd like to say I let myself escape into the book, all

thoughts of Jess and bathtubs free from my brain, but that, of course, would be a lie. Not even the greatest book ever written could keep me from thinking about her, imagining her hands running over her bare skin, soapy bubbles dotting the swell of her breasts, the strong lines of her calves.

I knew I should have jerked off.

I slam my eyes closed, as if that can somehow turn off my brain. Jesus Christ. I need to get it together. The last thing I want to do is make her uncomfortable, and if tonight has shown me nothing else so far, it's that Jess has zero interest in even talking to me, let alone reconciling in any way, shape, or form.

I've firmly resolved I will not think of her as anything but a colleague when the door to the bathroom opens.

More steam spills into the room, but it's not enough to cloud over what else emerges.

Jessica. Wearing nothing but a towel.

She looks at me sheepishly. "I didn't bring anything to sleep in."

She always did prefer to sleep naked, a fact that I'm remembering way too fucking late in the game.

I direct my eyes toward the ceiling so I don't ogle her. Reaching for the hem of the white T-shirt I'm wearing, I tug it over my head and toss it her way. When I don't hear the bathroom door close again and she doesn't say anything, I peek over at her.

Her eyes are glued to my torso. Actually, they're not glued, they're roving, skirting over my pecs and tracing down my abs.

I flex a little.

Her eyes finally meet mine and she realizes I've been

watching her watching me. I grin and her cheeks color, as red as the holly berries in the wreath hanging on the door.

She scampers back into the bathroom and I swear I hear the towel drop to the floor. I let out a silent groan, scrubbing my hand over my face.

Somehow, when she emerges once again, it's worse than before. My T-shirt barely covers the round curve of her ass. When she bends over to put her discarded clothes in her bag, I catch a tantalizing peek of skin, her underwear cut high enough to expose the bottoms of her cheeks.

From the slow way she returns to standing, I know this is my payback for flexing.

But if this is how she wants to get even, she can ogle me all she wants.

It's a familiar game, one we used to play often. Of course, back then it would end with the two of us wrapped in each other, naked and sated. Something tells me neither of us will be finding that kind of relief tonight.

She spins around, and the loose neck of the shirt—my shirt—slips from her shoulder, revealing a whole lot of collarbone. The thin white fabric does nothing to disguise the pebbled tips of her nipples.

I clench my hands into fists.

For a silent, heavy moment, we are at a stalemate, eyes locked on each other, neither wanting to be the first to move. Both of us refusing to be the one to acknowledge the thick tension.

She cracks first. "I can sleep in the chair."

"Don't be ridiculous." I pat the other side of the bed. "This bed is huge. There's room for both of us."

"I don't know if that's a good idea, Nick."

"Are you saying you don't think you can control your-self in bed with me?" I arch an eyebrow, poking at her be-cause it's fun and because I want her to be as affected by me as I am by her.

She rolls her eyes. "I'm not falling for your games, Nick Matthews."

"Ouch. Full naming me already." I lean back against the pillows, tucking an arm behind my head, watching as her eyes catch on the bulge of my biceps. "It's okay, I under-stand. I would be tempted by me too."

Her eyes narrow, and she stalks over to her side of the bed. "I am many things, Nick, but tempted by you is not one of them." She slips in between the sheets and turns her back to me.

And because she knows exactly what she's doing, she wiggles a little bit, causing the bottom hem of my T-shirt to ride up over the curve of her ass.

I stare for a second longer than I should before I roll onto my side, giving her my back in return. Reaching over to turn out the light, I plunge the room into darkness knowing there's not a chance in hell I'm going to be get-ting any sleep tonight.

"Good night, Jess."

"Night."

I must be imagining it, but her voice sounds a little breathy, like it always used to when she was getting turned on.

But that's the last thing I need to be thinking about.

So I close my eyes, wipe the vision of Jess's glorious ass from my mind, and pretend to fall asleep.

Chapter Nine

JESS

I am fully prepared to be met with a sleepless night, and so I'm pleasantly surprised when I feel myself drifting off, the exhaustion and the stress pulling me under. The bed is cozy, and the heat of Nick warms my back, providing a comfort I don't want to acknowledge.

Exhausted plus warm and cozy equals a fabulously deep sleep.

And even better dreams.

Many peaceful hours after climbing into bed, I feel myself drifting into the land of in-between, that moment when you're almost awake but not quite there yet, and I fight against it, keeping my eyes firmly closed and my breaths even and deep.

Because this dream is too damn good to leave behind.

A pair of strong arms encircles me, anchoring me against the hard plane of a chest. Fingers sweep over the bare expanse of my thigh, winding around, brushing against the exposed curve of my butt, teasing at the hem of my underwear for a hint of a second before they slide back up, under the fabric of my T-shirt, over my belly. The fingers skim my hip bones, somehow knowing the place where my hip and thigh meets is one of my favorite places to be touched. But the touch doesn't linger, tracing up to swipe the undersides of my breasts.

Dream me groans, my ass shifting back. The hard length of him presses against me, and dream me lets out a soft gasp.

I lean into it, lean into him, grinding my ass against his rock-hard cock.

My mystery man lets out a groan of his own, burying his face in the crook of my neck. I turn my head and my nose fills with the scent of pine and juniper.

Pine and juniper . . .

It's the familiar scent that yanks me out of the dream, thrusting me into the harsh reality where there will be no more thrusting and—ohmygod, was there really thrusting just now?

Somewhere in the space of the night, Nick managed to twine himself around me. I tell myself it was him, when I quickly realize we're actually in the middle of the bed and it's highly possible I'm the one who gravitated toward his warmth, toward the shirtless expanse of his chiseled chest.

But I refuse to believe even dream me would be so stupid.

Also, awake me needs to put a stop to this. Immediately.

But fuck it feels good, Nick's fingers hitting all of the spots he still, even after all these years, even in the muddled state of half-asleep, knows turn me on.

It's been a while since I've had a man in my bed, and I forgot how good it feels.

But no. This isn't right. Even if I did want to be wrapped up in Nick Matthews, which I clearly do not, the man is still asleep and obviously has no idea what he's doing.

"Nick." I place my hand on his forearm, the one currently locked around my waist, keeping our bodies pressed tightly together. I give his arm a little shake, but his only response is to find my hand and lace our fingers together.

He rocks his hips, letting out another groan, and he's so hard I want to reach in between us and stroke him.

Wait. What?

I definitely do not want to do that.

I turn over, repeating his name until his hazel eyes fly open.

In the few quiet moments before he realizes what's going on, he gives me a soft, sleepy smile, like this is right where he wants to be. Like this is right where we're supposed to be.

"Hi," he says, his voice croaky—and not at all sexy—with sleep.

"Good morning." I raise my eyebrows, looking down at our bodies tangled together.

Realization dawns in his eyes, and I start laughing at how quickly he scrambles away from me.

He pushes out of the bed so fast he almost face-plants on the floor. "Shit. Jess. I'm so sorry. I did not . . . I never meant . . . fuck." He plops onto the floor next to the bed, pulling his knees up to his chest, which can't be comfortable given the state his dick was in.

"It's fine. We were both asleep. Dream me was a willing participant."

He covers his face with his hands. "Still. You didn't want to share a bed with me, and I poked until you gave in, and then I went and did the exact thing you didn't want to happen."

"Are you sure 'poked' is the word you want to use there?" I attempt to lighten the mood with a joke, but when he doesn't laugh, I crawl across the bed, lying on my belly so the two of us are near eye level. "Hey. There was no malicious intent. We're two people who clearly used to be attracted to each other. It doesn't mean anything."

"I'll sleep on the floor tonight."

I hop up from the bed on the opposite side from where he's still hunched on the floor. "There isn't going to be a tonight, remember? I'm going home." I throw open the curtains, letting in the bright morning light.

Also letting in the reality that there is no way in hell I'm going anywhere today.

Thick blankets of snow completely cover the ground, and though nothing is falling from the sky at this current moment, it's an ominous sort of white, almost blending in with the ground below, which means it won't be long before it opens up and dumps on us once again.

"Shit." Nick has abandoned the floor and stands behind me. He echoes my unspoken sentiments.

"Maybe a room has opened up." I offer the suggestion half-heartedly, knowing all of the other hotel guests are trapped here just as I apparently am.

At that moment the phone rings, and Nick crosses the room to answer.

I tune out the conversation confirming what we already know, instead taking in the details of the room I tried to block out the night before. It really is an adorable little hotel, and if circumstances weren't what they are, I would love to be spending a night or two of the holiday season here.

Our room—Nick's room, I mean—isn't overly decorated, like they somehow knew he's an incognito Grinch. But there's a beautiful wreath hanging on the back of the door, and the blankets on the bed are a red and green plaid. There's a small wooden table next to the one armchair and on it sits a bottle of whiskey with a red bow tied around the neck.

I finger the tag, not caring that I shouldn't intrude on Nick's gift.

Congrats on Romance Author of the Year! You deserve the honor and many more. We're so happy to have you as a member of the SVP family.

The note is handwritten and signed by the president and publisher himself.

I force myself not to yank the tag from the bottle and rip it to shreds. Safe to say the publisher of SVP has never sent me so much as an email.

Nick clears his throat, and I turn away from the very expensive gift. In the meantime, I couldn't even get a room, let alone a bottle of booze.

"That was the front desk." Nick tugs on the longish hair at the nape of his neck, the move putting on full display the cut of his muscles. "It's still not safe to leave the hotel, but they're opening up the restaurant for meals, and we're welcome to use any of the facilities while we're here."

I nod, attempting a smile, though my lips seem to be frozen in place. "I think I'll get dressed and go downstairs then. I could use some coffee before I try to get some words in."

Thank god I brought my laptop, even though my original plan was only to be here for the one night. The one upside of being trapped here might be that it forces me to focus on my work in progress.

I also only brought one change of clothes, so I head into the bathroom and slip into my jeans and the chunky red sweater that gives holiday vibes without being overly Christmasy. After brushing my teeth and washing my face, I gather my laptop and the notebook I've been using to jot down ideas and possible plotlines for this manuscript.

When I come out of the bathroom, Nick is sitting in the armchair, his elbows resting on his knees, his head hanging down. Something about his posture screams defeated, and upset, but I don't give myself the space to care. Grabbing one of the keys from the dresser, I mumble a goodbye and head for the elevator.

I didn't get to explore much of the inn the day before, since I had to go straight to the party. But it's easy to find the tiny coffee counter, as it's got a long line of people streaming from it. I keep my head down in case there are any other SVP authors or employees waiting for their daily dose of caffeine. There have to be quite a few of us stuck here, though I'm sure some ducked out of the party early to escape the impending storm.

Despite the long line, it doesn't take more than a few minutes before my hand is wrapped around a steaming mug filled with chocolate-peppermint-flavored caffeine.

Nick drinks his coffee black, I remember, and just the thought makes my nose wrinkle.

But I'm not sure why Nick's disgusting coffee preferences should weigh on my mind. This is my one chance to put him out of my head, before we go back to being trapped in a cute little room at a cozy inn together. Which, of course, happens to have only one bed. Really, if I were still stuck for inspiration, this whole situation has all the makings of a romance novel.

Since it's us, it would be the Nick Matthews version of a romance novel: no happy ever after in sight.

I take my coffee and laptop over to one of the quiet corners of the lobby. There are tons of people milling around, everyone probably going a bit stir-crazy and looking for a little escape. But this section is separated from the main space, a tiny nook with a small café table and a perfect view of the Christmas tree that dominates the center of the room.

I use this small bit of privacy to check my phone for the first time today, knowing I'm going to need to find a way to spin this story to my friends so they don't completely lose their shit. Alyssa has already texted to check in, and I know I can't just leave her on read.

ALYSSA: How did everything go last night?!?! I need all the details immediately! Can we FaceTime later tonight?

KENNEDY: I'm around in the evening hours! Hope Nick wasn't a complete and total douchebag.

I groan, pinching the bridge of my nose, attempting to formulate a response. I decide to go with the basics—keep it simple and offer them nothing more than what they're asking for.

ME: The awards ceremony went about as well as can be expected. I made it through my speech and managed to get some face time in with the director of publicity, so it might have made the whole thing worth it.

ALYSSA: Amazing!!! That's such a great connection to have!!!

KENNEDY: And how was Nick? Did he make the whole thing super awkward?

ME: He was fine. We barely spoke to each other, which is probably for the best.

Of course, in between all the hardly speaking, there was a morning full of groping, but they don't need to know that.

ALYSSA: Are you back home already? Seems like the storm is still raging here!

ME: I'm actually still at the inn, waiting for the weather to clear. I'm going to get some words in while I wait out the storm and then hopefully I'll head home later today.

I know I won't be heading home, but they don't need to know that—at least, not right this minute.

ALYSSA: Yay! Let us know when you make it home so we know you're safe!

KENNEDY: And if you see Nick Matthews wandering the halls of the hotel today, tell him his books suck for me.

ME: Alyssa, I will do that. Kennedy, I'd like to not blow up any goodwill I gained last night so I will hold off on insulting my publisher's bestselling author.

ME: Love you both!

While I have my phone out, I send a text to Morgan letting her know I'm stuck at the hotel and, absent some kind of weather miracle, might miss my afternoon shift at the coffee shop tomorrow. Hopefully I'll be able to make it home in time because lord knows I can't afford to be missing shifts. Plus, as chill as Morgan is, leaving her hanging the week before Christmas is a bad look.

A shiver of fear runs through me as I think about what might happen if she had to fire me. I push that thought out of my mind. I need to manifest clear skies and getting the hell home, not just for my job's sake, but for my mental health's sake. I can't endure forced proximity with my ex for much longer. I am not cut out to be a romance heroine.

After shutting off my phone to prevent further distractions, I hunker down, sipping on my coffee as I read through everything I've written in this story so far. I haven't written in a few days—something I'd like to chalk up to the stress of the party and the weather, but really is more than likely due to a certain author who won't be named—and it helps to refresh my memory. I also use this time to flesh out any parts of the story so far that are lacking or need development. This method means it sometimes takes me longer to write, but it results in a first draft that is (usually) not a total dumpster fire.

And when it comes time to get some new words down on the page, I'm pleasantly surprised by the way they flow.

It's been about a week since I've been able to come up with anything new and I'm thrilled to find my mojo hasn't completely abandoned me. These characters have really come to life in my head, and it's easy to craft the banter, the banter that slowly shifts from combative to riddled with sexual tension to just plain sexual. The only thing I'm really struggling with is seeing how they reconcile in the end. How do they survive another breakup—the one that traditionally happens in the third act—without completely writing each other off? Are second chances in love really even possible?

But that's a problem for future me. I've just about written myself to the sex scene, a place where I know I will have to stop for the day because I am incapable of working on sex scenes in public, and even though my table is tucked away in the corner, there are too many other people around for me to be able to feel fully comfortable writing about throbbing cocks and peaked nipples.

I finish up the last few sentences, saving my document before I click over to the Internet so I can email myself the latest draft and also respond to any messages I might have. Though, of course, it's days before the holiday so publishing has shut down for two weeks and my inbox is empty.

Despite the cloudy skies, I can tell just from a peek out the window that it's still early afternoon and I can't imagine heading back to the room until I'm ready to climb into bed, needing to spend as little time in Nick's presence as humanly possible. But my options are pretty limited. I passed by a spa on the way to the barn yesterday, but I can't imagine they have any openings, and even if they did, I probably couldn't afford it.

Maybe they'll give me a discount since they totally fucked up my room situation. But something tells me that was likely an error on my publisher's part, not the hotel's.

I'm about to go grab a second cup of coffee when a familiar woman slides into the empty seat across from me.

"Lauren," I say, the surprise evident in my tone. I sit up a little straighter. "Good morning. Or is it good afternoon? I'm sorry, I've been writing and the time seems to have gone a little fuzzy."

She laughs, and it's as warm as this hotel lobby. "No problem. I think we're safely into the afternoon hours now. I take it you're trapped here like the rest of us?"

I nod, not sure if I want to mention the specifics of the situation. But then I open my mouth and it all comes out. "There was some kind of mix-up with the reservation for my room. They didn't have me in the system." I don't know why I decide to tell her; it's not like it's the publicity director's job to book hotel rooms for lowly authors, but something about her genuine smile makes me feel like she might actually care.

Her brow furrows. "I'm so sorry to hear that. I know it doesn't help much in the moment, but I will make a note to look into it further."

I shrug, a flush rising and heating my cheeks. "That's not necessary. It's no big deal, really."

"Where did you end up staying last night?" she asks with what appears to be real concern.

My face feels like it might actually be on fire. "Um, I stayed with Nick. We were checking in at the same time, and he heard about the whole mix-up so he offered to share his room with me. I would have texted Hannah but

I know she's sharing a room with Gina and I didn't want to intrude on their already-limited space." I'm babbling, an old nervous habit that I should have kicked a long time ago.

Lauren's eyebrows shoot right to the top of her hairline. "That was very kind of Nick."

I nod and purse my lips to keep myself from blathering any other information one of the highest of higher-ups definitely does not need to know.

"I know I mentioned this last night, but I never realized just how close you and Nick are."

"We've been . . . acquainted for a long time. I wouldn't say we're close, though." As long as you don't count this morning when we were practically dry humping each other.

"I don't know. I saw the way he was looking at you last night. It seems like there might be something more than a professional relationship there, if you know what I mean." Lauren sips from her own mug of coffee, watching me intently over the rim of her cup.

And dammit, this woman must have some kind of magical power, the kind that makes me feel comfortable enough to spew my deepest secrets. "We did date for a while, back when we were first getting our book deals. But it ended, and we haven't had much of a relationship since." My mind chooses that moment to fully digest her observation. "How was he looking at me last night?"

I tell myself I only care because I spent so much on that damn dress and I want to make sure I got my money's worth.

Lauren's sly smile lets me know I'm not fooling anyone, least of all her. "He couldn't take his eyes off you. If I'm not mistaken, there was a definite twinge of regret in those hazel eyes of his."

"They really are a gorgeous color, aren't they?" I respond before I can think better of it.

Seriously, what the hell am I doing here talking to the publicity director like we're besties giggling over some cute boy?

I clear my throat. "Anyway. I should be going. It was nice running into you." I don't have anywhere else to go, but I would rather go back to the room and spend the day watching Nick type than stay and continue this completely inappropriate and all-too-revealing conversation.

Lauren leans back in her seat, sipping from her coffee. "You know, I could spin a reconciliation between you two in so many ways. It would be publicity gold."

I freeze in place at her words. "I don't think a reconciliation is in the cards."

"Oh, I didn't mean to suggest anything like that." Lauren laughs, waving her hand in front of her face. "I'm just thinking out loud. I've been doing this job for so long I can't seem to turn off that part of my brain anymore. I see the PR angles in every situation."

I settle back into my chair, too curious for my own good. "I can see how pairing up with Nick would be good for me, but I fail to see how it would be beneficial for him too." Not that we will be reconciling or reconnecting or pairing up in any way. Certainly not in the way where our bodies meld together like they did this morning. That will not be happening again. Obviously.

Lauren glances around the room, like she's checking for spies. "Let's just say that the *pretty boy who writes tragic love stories* schtick is growing a little tired. The readers want something new, and different. The playboy bachelor is only attractive for so long. His audience is ready to see him in a new role."

I lean forward in my seat, floored by the direction of this conversation.

Lauren rises and waves nonchalantly like she hasn't just detonated a bomb in my chest. "But again, I'm just speculating, thinking out loud. I'm sure Nick will settle down when he meets the right person. Have a good rest of your day, Jessica."

I open my mouth to respond, but nothing comes out. What is there to possibly say?

And why does the thought of Nick meeting the right person, a person who isn't me, feel like I just found out there's no Santa?

Chapter Ten

NICK

The moment Jess leaves the room, the door shutting solidly behind her, I breathe for the first time this morning.

Fuck.

I can't believe what I did to her this morning, even if it was merely my subconscious that was being a total dick. Stroking her soft skin, nuzzling into her neck. Thrusting my rock-hard cock against the sweet curve of her ass.

Nope.

No need to visualize that one.

I push out of the armchair and grab my laptop, needing to turn my attention to anything but the memory of waking up with her in my arms. There isn't a great writing space here in the room, but I don't want to venture into the lobby. If I see her, it will only lead to distraction, and I need to get some words on the page before I lose this spark. I haven't felt this inspired for at least a week; the rush of my new story has been a temperamental beast.

I climb onto the bed, resting my back against the headboard and creating a pseudo desk with a stack of pillows.

I ignore everything I've written so far—I don't reread any of my writing until I completely finish the first draft—and dive in. My characters have taken shape, in my head at least, over the past twenty-four hours, and I know exactly where I want them to go.

I still don't know what broke them up in the first place, and it's unlike me to draft without fully understanding my characters' backstory, but I can't seem to find a good reason for their original breakup. They're so clearly suited for each other, there doesn't seem to be anything that could reasonably tear them apart. And if I can't settle on a reason for their breakup that seems reasonable and realistic, the readers will never go for it.

But I'm not going to worry about that now. There's one scene in particular that has been living in the forefront of my mind, and after this morning's events I can see it so clearly, I know I need to get it out on the page before I lose it.

I've always hated writing sex scenes, and it's one of the things that hasn't gotten any easier with time and experience. I know that romance novels don't need them; there are plenty of amazing closed-door books out there.

But when I was writing with Jess, well, a lot of times I would present her with a hypothetical—would this position work or what would happen if I did this to you?—and that hypothetical would lead to some of the best sex I've ever had, before or since. So I wasn't exactly shying away from putting as many sex scenes as I could think of into my books, not when it meant I would get to live them myself.

And now my readers expect sex to be there on the page. I still have to write it, only now it's without the benefit of a partner willing to act out the scenarios with me.

Today I don't really need to act anything out, the vision's so vivid in my mind that my characters' first time together comes pouring out of me. I type as fast as I can, the words barely keeping up with my train of thought.

I don't pause for a break, even though my throat has gone dry and my cheeks are flushed.

Jess barrels in, a wild expression on her face, and I'm so surprised to see her, am so wrapped up in what was happening on the page, I almost throw my computer across the room. Luckily, I have the foresight to save my work before slamming my laptop shut, as if there was some chance of her seeing what I was writing.

I wonder if I look as disheveled as she does as my breathing recovers from the shock of her walking in on me while I was consummating my characters' relationship. Her chocolate-brown hair, which she'd thrown up in a messy bun this morning, is now well beyond messy, like she's been raking her fingers through it.

I used to love raking my fingers through her hair.

I sit up, swinging my legs to the side of the bed. I take a deep breath so my tone is even and measured—the exact opposite of how I feel in the moment. "Everything okay?"

She opens and closes her mouth a few times, like she is struggling to make the thoughts in her brain connect with her mouth. Finally, after a few awkward pauses, she shakes her head. "Everything's fine." She stashes her own laptop back in her bag and collapses into the armchair.

I check the time. "It's going to be time for dinner soon. Should we go down to the restaurant and get something to eat?"

Her eyes widen. "Should we be seen together? There's still a ton of SVP people here."

My brow furrows with genuine confusion. "So? We're just two colleagues who happen to be trapped in a hotel during a snowstorm. We all need to eat."

She nods, her teeth pulling on her bottom lip. A sure sign she's got a million thoughts running through her mind that she can't quite untangle. "Right. Totally normal then, for us to go to dinner together."

"Are you sure everything is okay?" She's even more flustered than I am. I wonder what kind of scene she was writing before she burst back into the room.

She flashes me her fake smile. "Totally okay." She stands and heads for the bathroom. "Give me a few minutes to freshen up, and we can head down."

"Sure thing." My response gets swallowed up by the sound of the door clicking shut behind her.

While I wait for her, my eye catches on the gift bottle of whiskey. I find a glass and pour myself a finger's worth. I toss the whole thing back before Jess emerges from the bathroom, hair smoothed and tucked back into place. I focus on the burn of the alcohol sliding down my throat rather than how stunning she looks barefaced, her hair swept away from her cheekbones.

"Ready?" she asks.

I nod, not wanting to open my mouth and blurt out something inappropriate, like how when her red sweater slips off her shoulder, I want to lick her collarbone.

Because we are two colleagues, going out for a professional dinner.

I repeat it like a mantra in my mind, especially when the doors of the elevator close, and her winter jasmine perfume tickles my nose. It would be entirely unprofessional to hit the emergency stop button and press her up against the wall of the elevator.

Luckily, we're joined by two other guests as we hit the next floor, two people I don't recognize, thankfully.

We head directly for the restaurant, and the door opens right as we approach it. Two women emerge and their faces both light up when they spot me.

Scratch that. They're not looking at me, they're looking at Jess.

"Oh my god, Emily! Farah! It's so good to see you!" Jess's voice rises in pitch, as it always does when she's really excited.

The three of them huddle together in a group hug while I stand awkwardly next to them, clearly not included.

When they break apart, the blond one looks between me and Jess. "Are you two going in to eat? Together?" She says this like I'm the Grinch and Jess is Santa, like the idea of the two of us enjoying a meal together is near impossible.

"We are." Jess rolls her eyes as she leans in closer to them. "There was a whole mix-up with my room so I'm a little bit trapped."

"Oh no!" the brunette exclaims. "We would totally offer you a spot in our room, but instead of giving us two queens, they gave us one king, so we're already crowded."

Jess shrugs, and it's not lost on me that she doesn't

bother to introduce me or attempt to include me in this conversation in any way. "Hopefully I'll be on my way home soon. Fingers crossed this weather clears!" She pulls the two of them in for another hug.

"Are you okay?" I hear one of them whisper to her. "We can squish you in with us if you need us to. I can't imagine." She shoots me a glare over Jess's shoulder.

"I'm fine," Jess whispers back. I note she doesn't bother to defend my character. "Maybe we can all do a writing session tomorrow if we're still trapped."

Emily and Farah—I still don't know which is which—agree cheerfully before wishing Jess a good night, ignoring me, and striding toward the lobby.

Neither of us says anything as we put our name in with the hostess.

We wait in silence for a few minutes for a table at the cabin-themed restaurant. The place is full of wood beams and plaid and even some antique-looking wooden skis mounted on the walls. A giant Christmas tree stands in the center of the dining area, and holiday music pipes through the speakers. The fire is roaring in the huge stone fireplace, and the air smells like cinnamon and nutmeg.

It's awful.

One look at Jess and it's clear how much she loves it here. This place is exactly her kind of holiday vibe.

"So how long have you known Emily and Farah?" I finally ask, when the silence becomes too much.

She shoots me an odd look. "They debuted with us. I met them in the romance debut support group. We've been friends ever since."

Right. I was initially a part of that same group, but I

stopped participating once it became clear to me that I could no longer write traditional romance. But even still, I should probably have a general idea of who the other authors published by SVP are, especially the ones who debuted the same year I did.

"I don't ever see you in any of the SVP or romance groups . . ."

I purse my lips. "I've never really felt welcome."

"Maybe because it seems like you think you're too good for us." Jess drops the bomb right as the hostess calls our name.

If anything, I think it's the opposite. Emily and Farah and so many other romance authors have made it obvious that I'm not welcome in their circle, that *I'm* not good enough for *them*. The truly frustrating part is they're right. I know that I've brought their disdain upon myself.

Doesn't make it feel any better though.

The hostess seats us at a table right across from the tree, handing us menus and promising our server will be right with us. I already know I'm ordering the cheeseburger and a beer. Jess is going to get the grilled cheese with tomato soup and a glass of white wine.

I hide my triumphant smile when the waiter appears and she orders exactly that.

Food and drinks ordered and menus swept away, there isn't much left to focus on. Other than her.

"You look beautiful." It slips out before I can think of all the reasons I shouldn't say it.

Her full lips pull down in a frown. "I'm just in my hanging-out clothes with no makeup on. No need to try to flatter me."

I shrug, gratefully accepting the beer the server delivers. "I'm not. You just do, and I thought you should know."

She studies me for an uncomfortable minute before swigging from her glass of sauvignon blanc. "Thanks, I guess."

There's something new hidden in the depths of her brown eyes. Something different from disdain and lust, the only two emotions she's shown me since she arrived in a flurry the evening before. There's a whirlpool of emotion circling there, clouding her whiskey-colored eyes as she studies me.

Has it really been only twenty-four hours since she exploded back into my life?

Knowing I can wait her out, I drain half my beer.

"Did you ask SVP to have me introduce you last night at the awards ceremony?"

There's no judgment or anger in her question, just a genuine curiosity.

I shake my head. "I wouldn't do that to you, Jess. I know it can't have been easy to get up onstage and say nice things about me, but I also know it probably felt impossible to say no. I would never dream of putting you in that position."

"To be fair, I mostly said nice things about your books. Not that that's any easier than saying nice things about you."

I fight a smile as we slide into more familiar territory. "What's wrong with my books?"

She grimaces and finishes her glass of wine. "You claim to write romance, and yet, you completely disrespect one of the founding rules of the genre."

I sit back in my chair, ready for the debate I've had to

engage in many times over the years. "And yet, millions of readers don't seem to mind."

"It's not that your books are bad, Nick, or even that people are wrong for reading and enjoying them, it's that they shouldn't be marketed as romance."

I raise one eyebrow. "So you've read my books?"

She rolls her eyes and signals to the server for another round of drinks. "Obviously, I've read them, or I wouldn't know that you're incapable of writing a happy ending."

"How can I write a happy ending when my own blew up in my face?"

The shot of whiskey and the beer must have caught up with me because I can't believe those words just came out of my mouth. Shit.

"Blew up in your face?" Jess repeats, her voice incredulous. "You've got to be fucking kidding me. I seem to recall, vividly and explicitly, you being the one who ended our relationship. Unless . . ." Her eyes widen and she sits back in her chair, a humorless laugh caught in the back of her throat. "You're not talking about me. Of course, there was someone else."

My hand darts across the table, grasping onto hers. "There was no one else, Jess. There wasn't before you, and there hasn't been since."

She yanks her hand from mine. "Then why are you pretending like you're not at fault? Like someone else was responsible for the way we ended? Like you weren't the one who destroyed us?"

The server chooses this completely inopportune moment to deliver our second round of drinks, along with our food.

Jess glares at me for a second before pushing back her chair. "I think I'd prefer to enjoy dinner in my room." She takes her plate and the glass of wine and stomps out of the dining room.

Leaving me alone, the eyes of everyone in the restaurant watching me with either pity, or curiosity, or both.

I ignore the eyes and the hollow feeling in my chest, and eat my dinner. I text Hilary in total desperation, asking if she can work her assistant magic and find an extra available room in this fully booked hotel. It takes her an hour to respond, which means she really tried to work the system, but I'm not surprised when she tells me it's impossible. When I get back to the room, Jess is already tucked into her side of the bed. And she's left a mound of pillows down the middle of the mattress, making sure there won't be a repeat of this morning's groping session.

That mound of pillows might as well be a brick wall. Jess is never going to be able to forgive me. Our second-chance romance is over before it's really begun.

Chapter Eleven

JESS

I pretend to be asleep when Nick comes back to the room, and it's the most restful portion of the evening. How am I supposed to relax when I know what happened in the depths of my subconscious the night before? Sure, I built a wall of pillows between us this time, but something tells me my horniness and my intense attraction to Nick Matthews aren't going to let a little fluffy down get in the way of pressing against his rock-hard body.

And so, since I never really go to sleep, I make sure to "wake up" well before him. I dress in the same jeans and sweater as the day before, hoping today is the day the storm abates so I don't have to keep washing my bra and underwear in the sink. Though I did get a bit of sick pleasure from leaving my lacy red undergarments to dry in the bathroom, where there's no way Nick could miss seeing them. Payback for him noticing me ogling him the other night when he stripped off his shirt. If he wants to play the who'll-give-in-to-the-sexual-tension-first game, I'm a more than willing participant. I fully plan to come out on top.

Probably not the best way to phrase that, given the circumstances.

As quietly as I can, I grab my laptop and a key and let myself out of the room. It's still dark outside, and the coffee counter in the lobby is not officially open yet, but the barista takes one look at me and makes me a double peppermint mocha. Thank god for baristas.

Since there's no one else in the lobby save the lone employee behind the reception desk, I make myself comfortable in one of the cozy armchairs near the fireplace. The fire roars to life as I sit down, and my eyes fly to the employee, who holds up a remote and flashes me a smile. I return it and settle in to write.

But as so often has been the case lately, nothing comes. The previous day must have been a total fluke, probably brought on by something I don't want to acknowledge.

Okay, I don't *want* to acknowledge it, like even thinking about it might make it true, but I had the most productive writing session I've had in over a week. Right after waking up in Nick's arms.

I refuse to give weight to that thought, focusing my attention instead on the story in front of me. The second-chance romance that will end with an HEA, not the one I'm living where there will be no second chance and definitely no romance. I manage to get a couple sentences down on the page, but I know reading them back that they are going to end up getting cut.

But, I tell myself, this is why we have revisions. The important thing right now is to get something written. I can't edit a blank space, but between myself, my agent, and my editor, we can make even the roughest of rough drafts into a decent book. Hopefully.

And yes, I want more than just a decent book. I have dreams, plenty of goals still left unfulfilled. I'd love to hit a list or sell a movie option or be in some kind of fancy book box.

All things Nick has already done.

My eyes narrow on the screen, but I block him out of my head. This is my writing time, and I'm not going to let him intrude on my brain any further.

I stare at the screen for long enough that by the time I come up for air, the coffee shop line is snaking through the lobby and the restaurant is packed with breakfast goers.

Now that I've seen all the people, the noise of the room starts to seep into my brain. I'd blocked it out for a while, so lost in my own process—or lack thereof, if we're being honest—but now that I've heard the chatter, I know I won't be able to turn it off. I pack up my laptop, thinking I might grab some breakfast and maybe see about one of those massages.

My phone buzzes before I can abandon the noisy center of the lobby.

ALYSSA: Are you still alive? You were supposed to let us know when you got home safely last night!

Shit. I totally forgot, in the haze of my anger at Nick, to let my friends know I was still stuck here. It would probably be easier to tell them I'm back at home, but I can't lie to them, and something tells me I might need them to keep me grounded if I'm going to be trapped here with Nick for another few days.

ME: Yeah, so funny story. The storm is still going strong, and so I'm still here at the inn.

ME: And also, they lost my reservation and I don't exactly have a room because no one has been able to leave.

KENNEDY: So where the hell are you staying then?

ALYSSA: OMG!! Are you okay?!?!? I'm so sorry, Jess! I should have been there with you!

ME: You being here would just mean we are both trapped, I'm glad you're safe at home!

KENNEDY: Don't think you can avoid my question. Where have you been sleeping if you don't have a room?

ME: So funnier story. As I was attempting to check in, Nick was also checking in and of course they didn't lose his reservation so he offered to let me stay with him, so that's where I've slept for the last two nights.

My phone is still and silent for the next two minutes. Alyssa is able to get it together first.

ALYSSA: Are you okay?

Her simple question almost brings tears to my eyes. No judgment, just a desperately needed check-in.

ME: I don't know, honestly.

ME: Seeing him again has been a bit of a mind fuck. There's still *stuff* there. Attraction and feelings and lots and lots of anger.

ME: And to make it all worse, that publicity director I told you I met? She hinted that if Nick and I were to get involved, it would help both of our careers.

KENNEDY: Wait, what? She actually said that to you? Like she wants you to fake date or something?

ME: Okay, romance novelist. No, she didn't say anything as direct as that.

ME: Maybe I misunderstood her.

Maybe I willfully misunderstood her, not that I'm going to admit to that, or examine the thought too closely.

ALYSSA: How did Nick react to that?

ME: I haven't told him. She wasn't serious, so I figure it's not even worth bringing it up.

ALYSSA: Wow. That's a lot for just a couple of days. How are you holding up?

ME: I'm hanging in there. Just trying to keep a clear head. Last night at dinner Nick made it seem like he never wanted to break up with me, like he regretted the whole thing.

KENNEDY: Do you think that's true?

ME: I wouldn't have believed it, but Nick has never been a good liar, and there was something in his eyes that made me think he was telling the truth.

KENNEDY: Maybe this is the perfect chance for you to get some closure. Finally put him firmly behind you and let yourself move on.

ALYSSA: Or maybe this is the beginning of your second-chance romance! 🤩

ME: Absolutely not. That is definitely not what is happening here.

ALYSSA: Oh yeah? How many beds are in that cozy room at the inn you guys are sharing right before Christmas?

ME: I hate you.

KENNEDY: Alyssa, no. This is the man who straight up broke her heart. He doesn't deserve a second chance.

ALYSSA: Everyone deserves a second chance!

My stomach growls, reminding me that a double shot of caffeine and whipped cream is all I've had this morning—or is it afternoon? Time really doesn't seem to exist here.

ME: Let's put a pin in this convo. I'll check in with you guys later.

ALYSSA: Open your heart to love!

KENNEDY: Close your legs to ex-boyfriends!

Chuckling out loud at that one, I figure while I have my phone out I should also let Morgan know I might be MIA for a couple of days. For a second as I wait for her to answer, I worry about my job security, but she responds to my text almost immediately, assuring me she can cover my shifts, telling me to be safe and take care of myself.

I know the end goal is to someday not have to be a barista-slash-writer, emphasis on the barista, but I'm so glad if I have to have a day job, I have one like this.

My stomach growls again, and I make my way over to the restaurant. Given that everyone in the hotel is trying to get food from one spot, the place is packed. I know there's no hope of getting a table anytime soon and I'm about to abandon hope when I hear my name.

Hannah is waving from a table in the back corner, gesturing for me to come join her.

Thank god.

Except as I round the corner, I see Hannah isn't dining alone. Gina sits in the seat next to her. And Nick takes up one of the chairs across from them.

Of course. Gina is Nick's editor. How could I have forgotten that?

I plaster a fake smile on my face and slide into the seat next to Nick, shifting the chair so there is the maximum amount of space between us. "Hi, everyone. Thanks for saving me. I thought I was going to have to forage the vending machines for sustenance."

"Of course!" Hannah is way too bright and cheerful for someone who is snowed in at a hotel upstate just a few days before Christmas. "I wanted to chat with you about your new book idea anyway, so this is perfect!"

The last thing I want to do is talk about my enemies-to-lovers second-chance romance in front of my now-enemy, former lover who will not be getting any sort of second chance, but I think this is another one of those situations where I have to play nice.

Gina smiles over the rim of her coffee cup. "Perfect timing, Nick was just about to tell us about his new project too."

Nick shoots her a look like he was definitely not going to be doing that, but she just smiles and sips.

"So what are you working on?" Hannah asks.

"An enemies-to-lovers second-chance holiday romance." I say the words and then check the room because there seems to be some kind of echo.

It takes a second to realize there's no echo, there's just my ex-boyfriend stealing my book idea.

Okay. That might not be totally fair. Plenty of books have the same tropes while ending up being totally different from one another. But seriously, what are the odds?

My stomach sinks as I absorb the full impact of the situation, and I no longer feel hungry, only sick. There's no way my publisher is going to pick up my option if my proposed book is so similar to their stupid star writer's. This project of mine is grounded before it's even had the chance to take off.

Gina's eyes dart back and forth between us. "Wait a minute, you're both writing a second-chance holiday romance?"

I nod, keeping my eyes far away from Nick's. I can feel his gaze boring into the side of my head, but I ignore it, focusing instead on calming the nausea. Maybe if my book publishes a year after Nick's, SVP will still buy it. I can't really afford to go a whole year without publishing a book, but it might be the best offer I get at this point.

Nick clears his throat. "Yes. The idea came to me a couple of weeks ago."

My mouth goes dry. "Yeah. Me too."

Hannah and Gina exchange a look.

"How . . . how has that been going . . . for both of you?" Hannah's eyes are wide, like she's afraid of what we're going to say next.

"Fine," I say.

"Great," he says. "I've made a lot of progress."

I immediately know Nick has been struggling just as much as I have, that he's lying through his teeth. It makes me feel a teeny bit better. The nausea abates, replaced by the all-too-familiar sensation of being really, really annoyed with Nick Matthews. Why does everything between us always end up in a competition? My favorite thing about being a writer is my community of fellow authors. How much we love and support one another, how much we are there for each other. Nick has never wanted to be a part of that, and I hate how he holds himself at the top, without ever reaching a helping hand to those who make the community so special.

"It's weird though. I can't seem to picture how they come together in the end. I'm finding it hard to make the male main character's arc believable. Can he actually change? Could he truly make her happy the second time around when he failed so miserably the first?" I allow my gaze to drift Nick's way, just in time to see an angry flush darken his cheeks. "Why would she even want to give him a second chance when he fucked it up once already?" I normally wouldn't speak this way in front of publishing professionals, but one glance at Nick and I forget the need to hold back.

"Interesting. I'm struggling with figuring out my couple's backstory. The female main character seems to place sole blame for the breakup on the hero, even though she wasn't a completely innocent party. But she seems incapable of realizing how her own actions played a role in their split." Nick's eyes narrow as they meet mine.

"Maybe you should combine your stories and write a book together."

Both of our heads whip around, our gazes locked on Gina.

She shrugs. "Don't look at me like that. It sounds like you're writing similar books anyway. And you're both stuck at opposite ends. Plus, who knows how long we're going to be trapped here? Might as well accomplish something."

Hannah leans forward. "You know, it isn't a terrible idea."

"Isn't it, though?" My voice screeches loudly across the room, turning more than a few heads in our direction because I don't think I've ever, not once in my life, heard a worse idea.

"If nothing else, it might be a good exercise to get you both past the tricky parts. Even if the project itself doesn't turn into anything, maybe the brainstorming will unlock something about your current projects." Hannah is so smart and cool and yet in this moment, all I want is to punch her in the face.

Nick turns to me with a wide smile stretched across his face and my blood runs cold at the sight of it. "I think it sounds like a fantastic idea."

And there he goes, sealing my fate. Nick knows as well as I do that if he is on board to cowrite a book with me, even if it does turn out to be nothing more than an "exercise," there's no way I can say no.

What I can do is make sure he regrets his decision.

Chapter Twelve

NICK

have made a huge mistake.

Jess is pissed.

Jess is beyond pissed.

Jess is fucking livid.

The second the door to our room shuts behind us, I hold up my hands to ward off the attack. "I'm sorry. I shouldn't have said anything without checking in with you first."

"You think?" Her voice is so loud it makes me wince. "What the fuck, Nick? You think we can write a book together? You think we can just put everything that has happened between us aside and write a whole fucking book? *Together*?" She emphasizes the word with venom and menace.

"Okay. I'm sorry. I wasn't thinking. I didn't think it through." I keep taking the blame, knowing it's what she needs in the moment. Once she calms down—not that I am going to advise her to calm down because I'm a big fan of breathing, and I can't die while *Survivor* is still on the air—she's going to see that this is really the perfect solution. I want to point out all the reasons why this could work, lay out my argument with clear and precise logic, but it's not logic that's holding her back. It's feelings.

And maybe I'm a delusional fool, but I can't help but think that her emotions about the proposition are actually a good thing, for me. She doesn't trust herself with me.

Because she still has feelings for me.

But I don't let myself follow that train of thought, focusing instead on the work. The book we've both been working on, and struggling with, from the sounds of it. Between the two of us, it sounds like we have almost a whole manuscript already written. Obviously merging our stories is going to take some finesse and a lot of editing, but when we're done, we'll have a book. A damn good book, if I know Jess's writing.

She spends a few minutes pacing around the small room, muttering to herself. I sit on the edge of the bed and observe, trying not to smile because I know the turmoil she's working through right now is real, and she deserves to feel it.

She's just so fucking cute when she's angry.

I don't give myself the time to puzzle through what it is that I'm feeling in the moment. It's obviously not great that I went and did something to make her furious—again— but I still don't think I would change anything about the situation. Sure, there's a good chance that working on this book together doesn't bring us any closer to forgiving one another and moving on. But there's also a good chance that it does.

I don't keep track of the time, but it doesn't take as long

as I expect for her to collapse into the armchair with a defeated sigh. I open up my laptop, copying everything I've written so far and pasting it into a Google doc. Her phone chimes with an alert when I send her an email with the share link.

Glaring at me, she reaches for her own computer. A minute later, I receive a link to Jess's work in progress.

A tense silence fills every corner of the room as we read through what the other has written. I get lost in the story, in the world and the characters Jess has created, but that doesn't stop me from searching her face every so often as she reads my work. She tries to hide it, but I see the smiles, the suppressed giggles, the squishy eyes I know signal she's reached the point where the hero declares his love for his former girlfriend.

It should be unbelievable, how closely linked our stories are. But between our history and the DMs and everything unresolved between us, it's like we knew somehow this is where we would end up.

I was never one to believe in fate, but if I were arguing in support of it, this would be some compelling evidence.

"This is really good, Nick," she says, not entirely unbegrudgingly, an hour later.

"Thanks. Yours too." I move my computer to the bed so I can shift my position, so we're directly across from each other. "Your voice is so sharp, and your characters are perfect."

"Our characters are perfect, you mean."

So she caught that, that both of our female main characters are funny and sassy, with a supportive family and a clear sense of purpose. Our heroes are both more with-drawn, outsiders, with a sometimes-gruff attitude hiding a sensitive soul.

"If you really don't want to do this, you don't have to. I'll take the blame. Say the whole thing was my fault, and a terrible idea." I suck in a deep breath. "I'll write something else, come up with something completely different. Even if it means missing my deadline."

She looks up from her screen for the first time. "You would do that?"

"Of course." I try not to lose myself in the emotions swirling through her eyes. She was never very good at hiding her thoughts, especially not from me.

She sets her computer on the small side table, leaning forward, her elbows resting on her knees. "If we do this, Nick, I need for one thing to be clear."

"You have no intention of giving me a second chance." It hurts just to think the sentiment, let alone say it. But if the past couple of days have shown me anything, it's this.

I didn't come into this whole thing expecting a second chance. I didn't even know if I really wanted a second chance. I couldn't even allow myself to really want it, because I knew it would be so far out of reach.

And now I know, whether I want it or not, it's not on the table.

"I have no intention of giving you a second chance." She doesn't sound so sure, but I don't let myself linger on what could be wishful thinking.

"Okay."

"Okay." She nods, rubbing her palms against the tops of her thighs. "Let's get to work."

The next few hours play out like our own little movie montage. We start in separate corners of the room, communicating in grunts and eye rolls and the occasional sarcastic comment.

When Jess starts arching her back, I offer to switch places, letting her sit on the bed while I take the chair so she can be more comfortable but still keep the space between us.

But it doesn't take long before my own back starts aching. I'm accustomed to my ergonomic chair, and yes I know exactly how spoiled that makes me sound.

Jess watches me suffer for a few minutes before letting out a long sigh. "Just come back to the bed."

I do, cautiously, like she might change her mind and whack me in the face with a pillow. Because we're using the pillows to prop up our backs and our laptops, the barrier down the middle of the bed has disappeared, leaving just a foot of open space between us.

We write in silence for a few minutes.

"I really like the idea of the musical revue. It's a fun way to bring them together." It's a partial lie, I actually hate that part, would never dream of writing about something so outwardly cheesy, but Jess's unique voice—sharp and witty, fully indicative of her humor—has made it fun. And I need to say something to break the tension between us.

"Thanks. You've created some really good side characters. I love the family dynamic, especially the way the siblings interact with one another." She sounds like she actually means it too.

"Thanks." In the past, it was hard for me to write sibling relationships, since my own were so strained. But over the years, as the disappointment of me leaving Ohio and the family business has abated, it's become much easier for me to relate to my brothers, and for them to relate to me.

There's a few more minutes of quiet, each of us working in the Google doc, changing names and filling in missing details.

Jess stops typing, the silence much longer than it would be if she just needed to find the right word or come up with a transition. I chance a glance over at her and find her cheeks flushed a bright pink.

I scroll through the doc, finding her place and realizing exactly why she's so flushed. "Maybe we can work on the sex scene later?" I suggest.

"Yes, definitely," she agrees before I can even get the full thought out. She clears her throat. "But maybe this is a good time to talk about the ending?"

"The ending?" We're only about halfway, still have at least a dozen scenes to get through before we get to the final act.

She pulls her lip between her teeth. "All of my books have happy endings."

"But you've been struggling to see how this one would come together?"

She nods. "But that doesn't mean I feel okay with no HEA."

"My readers will be expecting the book to end with the couple not together."

"And my readers, like all romance readers, will be expecting them to overcome their problems and find a way back to each other." Her brown eyes meet mine. "The prob-

lem is, I don't know if that's realistic. Sometimes when people break up, it's for a good reason."

I pull in a calming breath, knowing this is about so
much more than what's happening on the page. "And
sometimes people need time to grow and change, before
they find their way back together."

She raises one eyebrow. "So you think this book can
end happily?"

I force my eyes back to the screen. "Honestly, Jess, at
this point, I don't know what I think."

It takes twenty-four hours, both of us working on different
sections of the now-combined manuscript, each of us taking turns raiding the almost-empty vending machines,
neither of us catching more than a couple of hours of sleep.
But by the evening of the next day, we have it.

It's still rough and probably riddled with plot holes,
and not actually finished—we haven't talked about the
ending again—but Jess and I have taken our two separate
stories and merged them into one.

She collapses into a heap on her side of the bed, slamming her laptop closed and shoving it (gently) to the floor.
"Are my eyes bleeding? They feel like they're bleeding."

I pretend to give her a cursory eye exam, really using
the time to unabashedly stare. "I think you've managed to
escape with both eyeballs firmly intact."

"What a relief." Her eyes flutter closed, giving me even
more space to watch her.

Okay. That sounds creepy, but I can't help it. She's got
that expression, the one that made me fall for her in the

first place. The creative spark is lit, and though she looks as exhausted as I feel, there's still a soft smile etched on her lips.

I jump up from the bed, knowing this train of thought can only derail and run into the side of a building and burst into an explosion of flames. "I'm going to use the bathroom. Want me to start the tub while I'm in there?"

"Ohmygod, yes. My hero." She groans and it goes straight to my dick, and I scamper into the bathroom before she can catch me.

I take way longer than I need to, waiting for the water to hit just the right temperature, filling the tub with the vanilla-scented bubble bath the hotel provided. When I open the door to the bathroom, she's standing right there and she looks so beautiful it makes my chest ache, and holy fuck what have I done? Writing this book together doesn't just mean spending the next few days hashing out plot points. It means copyediting questions and promotional appearances and signings.

More time with Jess trying to deny what's becoming more and more obvious.

I clear my throat, shoving down any and all traces of emotion. "All ready for you."

"Thanks, Nick." Her voice goes soft, and so do her eyes.

I make myself repeat the refrain. *She has no intention of giving me a second chance.*

I move out of the way, sweeping my arm in a wide arc like the fool that I am. "Your bath awaits."

She slips into the bathroom and closes the door behind her.

NICK

"Remember last Christmas?" Jess asks, laying her head on my shoulder and looking up at me with a grin.

I press a kiss to her forehead, settling back into the train seat so she can rest against me more comfortably. "How could I forget? You blurted out how much you love me in the middle of sex."

She swats at my arm half-heartedly. "It's not my fault your dick made me lose all sense of propriety."

"It is pretty potent."

She laughs, resting her chin on my shoulder. Her voice lowers to a throaty whisper. "Remember what I was wearing that night?"

I groan. As if it would be possible to wipe the memory of her lacy red lingerie from my mind.

She shifts a bit in her seat, and the movement gives me a peek down her V-neck sweater. Her breasts are encased in the red lace that has starred in more than one fantasy since this time last year.

I groan again. "Jesus, Jess. We're in public." I adjust my jeans. "Not to mention on the way to your parents' house."

"My room is on the opposite side of the house from theirs."

"I am not having sex with you at your parents' house."
Though fuck if just the thought doesn't make me half-
hard. I glance around the train to make sure no one is
looking our way.

She chuckles. "We'll see about that."

We both know I'm powerless to resist her.

It's been a year and a half, and the sex has somehow
only gotten better. I've never opened myself up to anyone
the way I've opened myself up to Jess, and who knew
being vulnerable with someone could actually lead to
orgasms so scorching I sometimes feel like my balls might
combust.

I'm one hundred percent certain this girl is the one.
And it isn't just the sex. It's everything between us. The
way we challenge each other, the way she makes me
laugh without even having to try. The way we both itch
to explore the world, but love coming back home. I never
really believed in soulmates, even though I write about
them, but Jess might be the one to fully convert me. It's
like the woman has no flaws.

"I love Christmas," she sighs happily, hitting me with
another punch-in-the-gut grin.

Okay, so she has one flaw.

I would never admit it to her face, but even her love
for the holidays is becoming a bit infectious. Like chicken
pox or herpes.

Jess's parents meet us at the train station and drive us
back to their perfect suburban home. I've met them
before, of course, but this is our first time spending the
holidays together, and it becomes abundantly clear from
the moment we pull into the driveway just where she

gets her love of Christmas from. Lights cover every inch of the exterior, and I'm blasted in the face with the smell of pine and cinnamon the second the door in the garage opens into the house.

Our upbringings were basically opposite ends of the spectrum, which has been a bit of an adjustment, but the Carringtons welcomed me into their lives with open arms, and I would be lying if I said I didn't enjoy the positive parental attention. I think they were almost as excited when I signed with my agent as they were when Jess signed with hers, coming into the city to take us both out for celebratory dinners. It helps that the Carringtons are extremely laid-back, there when we want them and need them to be, but fully happy to let us live our own lives.

When Jess announces over dinner that we're going to be moving in together, her mom squeals with delight, wrapping both of us in neck-crushing hugs. Her dad pulls me aside after the meal and I wait for a warning lecture that never comes. Instead, he tells me he's happy I'll be there to take care of her, that knowing she has me will make him sleep easier at night.

These feelings, so easily expressed and freely given, are foreign to me, but the more I get used to them, the harder it will be to give them up.

I force myself to halt that line of thinking. Jess and I have been going strong for a while now; there's no reason to think our relationship is going to end. If we could manage to get our books sold, our lives would be just about perfect.

But for the first time in months, I'm not thinking about selling my book. I push all publishing thoughts to the back of my mind as we enjoy dessert and open presents—my stack almost as big as the one for Jess and just as thoughtful—as we all sit around the tree, enjoying the warmth of the fire and a good glass of wine, playing the competitive card game we gifted her parents. The conversation flows easily, as does the laughter, and I think that maybe, if I'd grown up in a home like this, I might love the holidays too. In my house, the holidays were more about outward appearances than enjoying one another's company.

Not that my upbringing was bad, by any means. My parents provided for me and my two brothers. We never went without anything we needed, and we got most of what we wanted. I just never fit in. I was a leftist in a family of conservatives, my beliefs ostracizing me from them on more than one occasion. My brothers spent their early lives devoted to sports and working for my dad's construction company, while I spent my free time reading and writing romance novels. To their credit, they never made fun of me, or tried to change me. They just didn't understand me, could never understand why I would want to go away to college when I already had a job waiting for me.

The more space I've had from them, the easier it's been to accept our relationship for what it is. We don't get to choose our family, and maybe I was just born into the wrong one. I hold no grudges; I pick up the phone whenever they call. Should any of them need me, I would be there in a heartbeat. Someday, I would like to make them proud, prove to them that moving to New York and pursuing writing was the right call, but for now, we aren't friends. And that's okay.

That doesn't mean the hints of envy don't creep in every once in a while, when I watch Jess with her parents. They all genuinely enjoy each other's company, and sometimes I wonder what that might be like. But mostly, I just feel lucky that I get to be a part of this family, for however long they'll have me.

After Jess's parents have headed up to bed, Jess cuddles up next to me on the couch. I finish my glass of wine, my hand finding hers. I absently play with her fingers, and it isn't until she chuckles that I look down and see that I've created a sort of ring around the ring finger of her left hand.

"Not yet," she tells me with a smile.

"But someday."

"Someday," she concedes.

"I love you, Jessica Carrington. You are going to do great things in this world, and I'm just lucky to be along for the ride."

She tilts her head up and places a soft kiss on my waiting lips. "I love you too, Nick Matthews. And we're going to do great things together. Side by side."

I deepen the kiss, unable to hold myself back.

"Let's go upstairs," she whispers, a waggle in her eyebrows.

The door to her childhood bedroom closes behind us and Jess reaches behind me to turn the lock, not that her parents are the type to disturb us. Her room no longer reflects teenage Jess, the purple walls have been painted a soft gray, the boy band posters replaced with framed family photos. But there are still remnants of her here: the stuffed panda that sits at the head of the bed, the first short story she published in her high school's literary magazine displayed on the wall.

"I know you have some sort of moral issue with fucking me in my childhood bedroom, but I really need you to get me off, Nick." She mutters the words against my lips, already reaching for the hem of my sweater and tugging it over my head. She removes her own sweater next, showing off her perfect tits framed by that damn red lace.

"You know I'm powerless to refuse you." I guide us over to the bed, sitting on the edge and pulling her onto my lap.

"I know." She grins wickedly, and my dick throbs in my jeans.

She rolls her hips slowly over my hardness as I lick along the edges of the lace of her bra, flashbacks from the year before dancing in my head and driving me too close to release—but I've just gotten started. Her head falls back as I cup her breasts, rubbing my thumbs along her nipples and biting gently at the spot where her neck meets her shoulder.

"I can't wait," she says, jumping up from my lap to shove her jeans and underwear to the floor. She moves to unclasp her bra.

"Leave it," I growl, unzipping my own jeans.

She climbs back into my lap, taking my cock in her hand and guiding me into her slick heat. I work her nipples through the lace of her bra while she rides me. My thumb finds her clit, stroking her the way I know she likes it.

She moans, and I move my mouth to hers, swallowing her cries as she tightens around me, her release rolling through her, her head falling back like she can barely hold herself up. I flip her to her back, and she hooks her knee over my hip as I stroke into her. Louder, more desperate sounds escape her, and I cover her mouth with my hand.

"Okay?" I ask. I've never restrained her in any way before and I need to check in.

Her eyes widen and she nods.

"Pinch my forearm if you want me to stop."

She nods again, but I can tell from the way her eyes darken that she's enjoying this, enjoying me taking control in this situation. Something about the trust she puts in me, the way she gives herself over completely, unlocks something deep inside my chest. She looks so fucking gorgeous beneath me that it doesn't take long before the familiar heat starts low in my belly. I pump into her, delighting in the muffled cries she releases against my hand.

"Can you come again?" I choke out, only barely holding myself back.

She nods, clutching me closer to her. I slam into her, grinding how she likes, and she clenches around my cock. I pull my hand from her mouth just in time to kiss her as the orgasm rips through me.

I soften my kisses as she strokes her hands through my hair and down my bare back, as I realize there is no place on this earth I would rather be in this moment, and no one else I could ever be with.

"Best Christmas ever?" she whispers.

"Best Christmas ever," I agree.

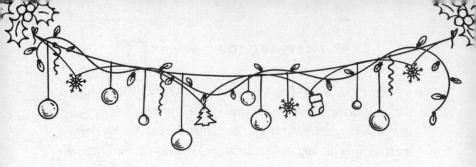

Chapter Thirteen

JESS

The bath is warm and nothing short of heavenly. I sink into the water, closing my eyes as if it's going to block out everything that's happened over the past twenty-four hours.

I hate to admit it, won't ever admit it even if someone asks, but it was so easy to fall back into old patterns once I accepted the inevitable. Of course writing a book with Nick sounds like it would be tantamount to torture, but I would be a fool to ignore what this could do for my career. I vowed to make him hate working together, but I forgot that part of the mission after the first five minutes.

I didn't expect the whole process to be fun.

Of course it's only been one day. There's still plenty of time for things to go downhill.

But I don't think about those possibilities. I enjoy my bath, dressing in Nick's shirt and sliding into bed, the pillow barrier between us still firmly in place, maybe more necessary now than ever.

I say good night and turn out the light, and the events of the past day catch up with me, allowing me to slip into a blissful sleep where I definitely do not dream about Nick Matthews.

I wake the next morning before Nick, using the opportunity to sneak out of the room before he opens his eyes. I make my way down to the lobby, keeping my fingers crossed for some good news.

The grumpy-looking older man behind the counter of the reception desk does not look like he is going to be the bearer of good news. I've spoken with him before, and though I wouldn't have described him as friendly, he certainly didn't give the impression that I was the bane of his existence—the glare he greets me with this morning tells me things might have changed.

"Hi," I say, flashing him the brightest smile I can manage after three days trapped in this inn. "I don't suppose there's any chance of the roads reopening today, Stanley?" I throw in the name on his tag. I always like it when customers at the coffee shop take a moment to remember that I am a human being and not just a vessel delivering their drinks.

Rather than answering my question, he looks out the front windows of the lobby. Pointedly.

As I have yet to check the weather outside this morning, I glance over his shoulder and see nothing but white. "Right. Guess that's a no. In that case, I don't suppose there's any rooms that have opened up since Saturday?"

Now that Nick and I are going to be working together for the foreseeable future—I wait for a wave of nausea to overtake me, but instead there's just a warmth spreading through my veins—I need some distance from him. It would be so easy, too easy, to fall back into our old habits, and if I'm going to survive this project and avoid any hint of reigniting the old flame that needs to stay dormant, space is going to be a necessity.

The man's look can only be described as withering, even after I went through the trouble to learn his name. "Given that no one has been able to leave, that would be a no. Still a no, no matter how many times you all check."

"Right. I figured it didn't hurt to ask." Though it did seem to pain him, greatly. "One last question."

"Can't wait."

"Are there any appointments today for a massage? Assuming the spa staff are trapped here like the rest of us?" I try my charming smile one more time, but this man is unbreakable. Apparently the past few days have killed his holiday spirit.

"Room number?" he asks with nothing less than disdain.

I give him the number for what's technically Nick's room and low-key hope he'll charge the massage to the room without my having to ask. Nick owes me a minimum of a massage and it's not like I'm *asking* them to put it on his tab. I would just be totally okay with it if it happened to shake out that way.

"All right, ma'am, you have a two o'clock massage."

"Amazing." I don't bother to ask for pricing because something tells me he either doesn't have the information, or isn't willing to give it. So even though I know it's probably out of my budget, I make the executive decision to put it on my credit card and make it a problem for future me. "Thank you."

Spa session booked, I thank Stanley again for his oh-so-helpful assistance and head to the coffee counter for some sustenance and a quick breakfast. The pastry case is looking very sad compared to its offerings just a couple of days ago, but I manage to snag a bagel and a table in the corner of the lobby.

I open the Google doc, going back to the beginning so I can read through what we have so far. It's hard to believe that between the two of us we have almost a complete book. There's still no ending, and still no answer to the million-dollar question—is this book ending happily or not? I will fight for the HEA with everything I have, but something tells me if Nick wants this book to end in a split, he gets to be the deciding vote.

I avoid thinking about it for now. Instead, I spend my time today focusing on layering in the backstory, the reason our two characters broke up the first time around. It's a delicate balance with a second-chance romance. You want the reason for the breakup to be believable, but neither of the characters can do something entirely unforgivable. And even though plenty of couples in real life suck at communicating, readers hate when a simple miscommunication is responsible for the split.

I don't notice when Nick shows up in the Google doc, not until he highlights a sentence I've just written, when the hero cowardly walks away without explaining his feelings, and adds a comment.

Maybe he was just scared. Maybe with all the career changes and life changes he's going through, this relationship was just too much for him.

My forehead furrows as I type my response. **That's a cop-out.**

I think it's a valid emotion, he types back. Also, there are so many layers to this from his perspective. He's got the weight of his family's expectations, plus the pressure of living up to these new career demands.

So that makes it okay for him to dump her without an explanation?

It doesn't make it okay, Jess, but that's not what we're doing here. We're uncovering the reasons why they split, not defending their choices.

He's right, not that I would ever say—let alone type—those words. This isn't about our opinions on our characters' breakup, it's about giving their story depth of feeling.

I'm going to take a break, he tells me before signing off, and it doesn't escape me that once again Nick is walking away right as things are getting emotional.

I check the time and see that I need to get a move on as well if I want to be on time for my massage. I head back up to the room, needing a shower before I let some stranger put their hands all over my body. I say a quick prayer outside the door that Nick has vacated the room and somehow we just missed each other down in the lobby.

For once, the gods or the Fates or whoever the hell is in charge these days seem to be on my side. The room is blissfully empty when I peek inside. I'm tempted to take another bath, but two in the span of twelve hours might be a lot, even for me. My skin is going to be pure prunes by the time I finally get out of this hotel.

I let the warm water run over me, turning up the heat until my skin flushes bright pink under the stream. I use the time to try to center myself and anchor my thoughts. Make sure I remember the difference between fact and fiction, between what's happening between our characters and what's happening between us.

Because there's nothing happening between us, and that's how it's going to stay.

I would hope that if Nick had returned to the room while I was in the shower, he would have knocked on the closed bathroom door to let me know, but I still tiptoe into the room fully dressed after my shower, just in case. Luckily, he still hasn't returned, and since it's almost time for my massage, I head back to the lobby, thankful we seem to keep missing each other today. It might not be the kind of space I really need from him, but it's space nonetheless and I'll take what I can get.

An unfamiliar person at the front desk directs me to the spa the back way, since the main path to the building requires going outside and I have zero desire to do that. I check in at the front desk of the spa and am directed to the locker room to change into the soft and cozy robe I find waiting for me in an assigned locker. The changing room is quiet and peaceful, and I allow myself a few moments to breathe before I slip my feet into the spa-issued sandals and head into the waiting area.

"Jessica?" The deep voice of my masseur startles me, even though he's kept the volume down to preserve the sanctity of the spa.

"That's me," I squeak, as I take in the behemoth of a lumberjack in front of me.

He's huge, at least six foot five, with muscles bulging out of the scrubs-like uniform he wears. His long hair is tucked into a man bun that I should hate but really don't, and despite my general aversion to bushy facial hair, I've never seen a beard more attractive than the one on his perfect face.

I gird my loins, wait for the attraction to hit me, wait for my reserved-for-flirting smile to take over my face, but there's nary a stirring down in the nether regions.

Hmm.

Wonder what that is all about.

"I'm Jake, I'll be your massage therapist today. If you'd like to follow me, your partner has already checked in for your couples massage."

I'm so enraptured by the timbre of his voice, it takes me almost a full minute of following him down a long hallway before I register what he just said. "Wait a minute, did you say a 'couples massage'? I didn't ask for a couples massage. I couldn't, as I am not currently a member of a couple. Who could even be coupled with me for a couples massage?"

My word vomit stops the minute Jake opens the door to the treatment room and I see the other half of this nightmare.

Nick stands next to a massage table, dressed in a matching robe and sandals. The robe has come open at the chest, leaving his smattering of chest hair and defined pecs on full display. Probably for the benefit of the drop-dead gorgeous woman standing next to him, dressed in a uniform identical to Jake's.

Nick's eyes go wide when he sees me, but he doesn't say anything, doesn't do anything to put a stop to the madness.

"Excuse me, but I think there's been some kind of mistake. This was supposed to be an individual massage." I turn pleading eyes to Jake, who exchanges a glance with his supermodel counterpart.

Jake pulls out a tablet and taps a few clicks on the screen. "You are Jessica, correct? Staying in room 323?"

"Yes, that's me."

"And you're Nick, also staying in room 323?"

Nick nods, and I urge him with my eyes to speak up and freaking do something, but he ignores me.

"We are sharing a room," I continue to protest-slash-explain, "but we are not a couple. Can my treatment be moved to a separate room?" There is no way I can lay next to Nick, naked and separated by a mere few inches, for the next fifty minutes while Jake's massive hands knead the stress from my body.

"Unfortunately, all of our other rooms are booked. And Chelsea and I specialize in couples massage. It would be difficult to change the program at this point."

I shoot daggers at Nick. Is he smiling? What the fuck could he possibly find funny about this hellhole of a situation? This might be worse than waking up next to him in bed.

"Come on, Jess." He finally breaks his silence. "It's just a little massage. How bad could it be?"

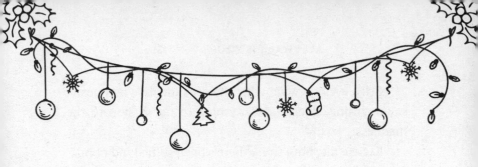

Chapter Fourteen

NICK

I put on my smirkiest of smirks, but on the inside, I'm about to go into full-throttle meltdown mode. When I asked Hilary to book me a massage, this is not what I had in mind. How the fuck am I supposed to relax with Jess lying six inches away from me, completely naked while another man rubs his hands all over her body?

But she's so utterly freaked out by the idea of this couples massage that I feel like I have no choice but to pretend like it's no big deal. Like I want nothing more than to watch someone else lotion up his hands and work the kinks from her shoulders.

I swallow thickly.

She glares at me.

I realize too late this is the second time in as many days that I've pushed her into something she doesn't want to do. I open my mouth to let Chelsea know I don't need a massage after all. Let Jess have her moment with Jason Momoa's twin brother, even though the thought makes me want to hurl.

But Jess speaks before I can. "Now that I've had a

second to think about it, a couples massage sounds great. Should we take our robes off now?"

Something seems to have lodged itself permanently in my throat because no matter how many times I swallow, I can't seem to catch my breath.

Chelsea and Jake exchange a round of nervous glances.

Finally, Chelsea clears her throat. "We'll step outside so you can disrobe in private. Take your time and get comfortable on the massage tables. We'll have you start face down, please."

The two therapists scamper from the room, and I can only imagine the conversation they're having about us in the hallway.

The door clicks shut and Jess immediately turns up the heat on her glare. "I cannot believe you! How can you be so nonchalant? I can think of nothing I want less than to have a fucking couples massage with you!" She huffs, crossing her arms over her chest, and it's so cute I almost make a life-ending mistake and smile. "Just because we're writing this book together doesn't mean things can just go back to the way they were, Nick."

"I know that, but this appears to be a genuine misunderstanding." I shrug like my heart isn't pounding out of my chest, like this stupid massage didn't just destroy whatever progress we've made. "We're here, and there's nothing we can do about it now, so we might as well try to relax and enjoy."

And since we're here about to get a fucking couples massage, then now is the time for me to take full advantage of the situation, make the next move in this undeclared, sexual-tension-laden chess match we've been engaged in over the past few days, starting with that fuck-me red dress. I move my hands slowly toward the belt of my robe, making my intentions clear and giving her plenty of time to turn away. She wants to leave her lacy red bra and thong draped over the shower door for me to find in the morning? Well, two can play this game.

The pulse flutters in her neck and the internal debate plays out over her face. Her eyes drop to my waist, and if she wants a show, well, I don't plan on denying her.

This attraction between us has been flaring since the moment I saw her. For the past three days, I've had nothing but reminders of how my body reacts to hers, longs for hers, aches for hers.

And as much as she tries to hide it, I know she wants me too.

I let my robe hit the floor.

She sucks in a little breath, a hint of a gasp.

At some point she gives up the ruse and straight up ogles me, her eyes tracing over my chest, down to my feet, then back up, lingering for so long on my dick that I'm half-hard by the time her gaze travels back to my face.

I arch one eyebrow in a silent challenge.

Her hands flutter around the tie of her own robe, but she hesitates, and the last thing I want is to make her uncomfortable. This game we're playing is a dangerous one, and I don't want to push her so far that she quits before I've won.

I slip between the sheets of my massage table and turn my head in the opposite direction. I hear the soft whomp of her robe hitting the floor and have to reach down to adjust myself at the sound of her skin sliding against the sheets.

"Thank you," she says softly.

I take that as my cue and turn my cheek to face her. Which is a mistake because she is right there, close enough that it wouldn't take much to close the gap between our mouths. And from the soft look in her deep brown eyes, I don't think she would stop me.

A knock on the door keeps that thought from intruding further.

Jake and Chelsea reenter the room, each of them coming to one of our sides. There's some adjusting of blankets, and Chelsea puts some kind of pillow underneath my feet.

"Normally, we incorporate some relationship exercises into our session, to help our couples connect with both body and mind." Chelsea's voice is soothing, so quiet and peaceful she probably puts many clients to sleep. "Would you like us to skip those exercises today?"

I'm about to tell her she absolutely should, but Jess answers first. "Actually, I think we could really benefit from some of those exercises, to really help us get in touch with our emotions. Don't you think, Nick?"

This time I'm the one glaring, and if this is supposed to be payback for the free show I just put on, well, that would mean she would have to be pretending like she didn't love every second of it.

"Nothing I love more than getting in touch with my emotions," I grind out from between gritted teeth.

"Fantastic!" Chelsea exclaims in her melodic voice. "Let's get started."

Chelsea's warm hands land on my shoulders a few seconds later, slick with some kind of oil that smells like eucalyptus and lemon. My eyes flutter closed, happy to have a reason to not have to stare directly at Jess. Looking at her this close is like looking directly into the sun. I don't mean to let the groan escape when Chelsea digs into the knots of my upper back, but it slips out anyway. I spend my days sitting in front of a computer; my back is a wreck.

For a few minutes, there's quiet, nothing but the sounds of the ethereal music and the occasional brush of movement as Chelsea and Jake continue our massages.

Then Chelsea breaks the silence, and even her soothing voice isn't enough to make what's going to happen next any easier. "Why don't we start with each of you saying one thing you admire about the other?"

I pry my eyes open in time to catch the regret flashing through Jess's eyes. I smirk, because she brought this on herself. She wanted to "get in touch with our emotions" and now she's going to be forced to say nice things about me.

"I'll go first," I volunteer, because I know it will annoy her even further. "The easy compliment would be to point out the obvious—Jess is nothing short of gorgeous. But really, part of what makes her so beautiful on the outside is the positive light she carries on the inside. She is kind and generous and is always willing to go out of her way to do nice things for others."

It's all true, of course, but I deliver the words with a tilt of a sarcastic smile, just to get in her head.

"That was lovely," Chelsea praises, right as her elbow digs into a knot in my shoulder. "Jessica?"

Her eyes look everywhere but at me, which is kind of impressive given how close our faces are to each other. "Nick is a good writer."

No one says anything for a minute, giving her the space to elaborate, which obviously she chooses not to do.

"Okay, great," Chelsea says after an awkward pause. She blesses us with a few more minutes of peaceful silence before delivering the next question. "Now, why don't each of you tell the other what physical trait you find most attractive in the other?"

"His eyes," Jess says immediately, the answer flying out of her mouth before I even have the chance to think of my response.

In reality, I find every inch of her attractive, from her thick dark brown hair, to her wide smile, to the body that haunted my dreams even before we were stuck sharing a bed. But that's a cop-out, and so I narrow in on something a little more specific. "I love her skin. How soft it is, and how it flushes whenever she's embarrassed or . . ." *Aroused*, I think but don't say out loud.

Those cheeks are bright pink at the moment, probably due to a combination of both emotions.

"Fantastic." Chelsea rewards us with a break from questioning, though she uses that time to dig into the muscles of my upper back. I'm going to be sore tomorrow, but it feels amazing in the moment.

While we all sit in the quiet, I crack one eyelid, just a smidge. Jess's eyes are fully open, watching me with an unreadable expression on her face. I blink my own open all the way, meeting her gaze full on. I would give just about anything to know what she's thinking right now.

She searches my eyes, then lets her gaze wander. Both of us are bare to the waist, where Jake and Chelsea have tucked the sheets low around our hips. The very top of her ass is exposed, and since she is taking the opportunity to look me over, I allow myself to indulge in the same.

Our eyes come back to each other's just as Chelsea delivers her next question. "What is your favorite memory of the other person? Nick, why don't you go first?"

I hesitate, forcing myself to shuffle through the memories like songs on a playlist. The one that's my real favorite is one I can't mention. I wasn't even really there to experience it with her, so I'm not sure it counts anyway. But nothing could ever top watching Jess sign her first book deal and publish her first novel. I had to watch from the sidelines, through Instagram and blog posts, but seeing her dreams come true, well, it was everything.

"I can go first," Jess offers, and I'm not sure if it's hurt in her voice or understanding.

Does she think I can't think of a single favorite memory, or does she know there are just too many to choose from?

"Our first Christmas together was my favorite. We were still newly dating and we stayed home, just the two of us. We ordered Chinese and watched Christmas movies. I know you never liked the holidays, but I loved that you were willing to put up with it because it was important to me."

My heart seizes in my chest. I never did like the holidays before I met Jess. And after I lost her, they became one of the most painful times of the year for me. But I loved that first Christmas together too.

"That was one of my favorites too." But I can't piggyback onto her happy memory, so I pull a random one from a hat. "I loved traveling with you, everywhere really, but I think our trip to Scotland was my favorite." It's not a lie. Some couples are terrible at traveling together, but it was one of our favorite things to do. We had plans to see the world together.

A small smile pulls on her lips. "That was a good trip."

For a too-short second, we share a grin.

Then Chelsea and her impeccable timing strike again. "Lovely. Now we're going to have you turn on your backs and we'll adjust the tables."

Chelsea holds the sheet up for me like some kind of shield, but it doesn't do much, at least not if what's happening a few inches from me is any indication. Jess flips over onto her back and in the brief few seconds, I catch a glimpse of everything. The smooth line of her spine, the dip of her waist, her rosy pink nipples, and the flushed skin of her chest.

And then the table beneath me starts to roll, and the already infinitesimal gap between us closes. Our massage tables are now pushed together to form another single fucking bed. It's like the romance gods are trying to murder us.

The tables aren't big to begin with and this new arrangement means my bare shoulder is pressed against Jess's, that silky skin I'm so obsessed with brushing against mine with every inhale. And then Jake and Chelsea adjust the sheets, so that our hips and thighs and hands and so many parts of us are touching that I might actually combust.

Whoever invented couples massages should be forced to endure the worst kinds of torture. Riding "it's a small world" at Disneyland for days on end, or going through copyedits on sex scenes.

Chelsea's hands are working my neck muscles, but the only thing my body is aware of right now is Jess. She is everywhere, and I want more.

I move my pinky finger, half a centimeter by half a centimeter, until I finally feel the brush of her skin on mine. It's innocuous and could easily be passed off as an accidental touching, almost unavoidable given the circumstances.

And yet, when she moves her pinky, just a smidge, so that it's underneath mine, when I take the chance and wrap mine completely around hers, she doesn't pull away.

I release the breath that's been trapped in my lungs since the table moved and the earth shook.

"One last question," Chelsea says. "Tell each other one thing you regret most, something you've said or done that you would take back if you could."

I turn my head, searching for her eyes. "The end. All of it. I regret everything about the end."

She meets my eyes and hers are shining with tears. I let go of her pinky so I can take her hand in mine. I squeeze gently, and she grips my fingers with equal force.

"I don't think I can do this," she whispers.

I swallow the threat of my own tears and nod. "You don't have to."

There's a beat of heavy silence before Jake speaks for the first time since our massage/torture session started. "Take your time getting dressed. We'll meet you in the hall whenever you're ready."

Jess and I both nod. Neither of us moves when we hear the door click shut behind them.

I reach out a tentative hand, tucking a lock of her dark hair behind her ear. "I really mean that, you know. I regret losing you every day, Jess. I hate how much I hurt you. And I hate that I now have to live without you."

A tear slips down her cheek. "Then why did you do it?"

I grimace, because of course she wants to know the one thing I don't think I could possibly explain. "I don't have a good answer for that, Jess."

She gently pulls her hand from mine, wiping at her cheeks. She holds the sheet to her chest as she rises from the table and gathers her robe from the floor.

I look away as she dresses, as if giving her a smidge of privacy could possibly make up for the thing I can't give her—the truth.

"You know, Nick, I don't regret anything about our relationship. I loved you fully and completely, and the years that we spent together were some of the best of my life."

I sit up, letting the sheet fall to my waist as I face her. I owe her that much at least. "I agree, Jess, and I loved you too, even if it didn't feel like it at the end."

She shakes her head sadly, toying with the ties of her robe. There's no teasing sexual tension in it this time. "I lied, actually. I do have one regret. I regret whatever it is that makes you think that you can't trust me with the truth."

She doesn't give me a chance to respond, not that I could find the words anyway.

I watch her helplessly, silently, as she walks from the

room and closes the door behind her. Scrubbing a hand over my face doesn't wipe the memories from my brain, or her words from my heart. I dress in my robe and thank Chelsea for the massage and change back into my clothes in the locker room.

I ask at the front desk if there are any extra rooms available, knowing full well there won't be. Stanley, the same hotel worker from the first day, has gotten even grumpier over the course of being trapped at his job, and he seems to delight in telling me my "girlfriend" already inquired about moving to a new room. Of course there aren't any open rooms. I knew that, and yet, it still feels like a blow.

I don't know how I can climb into bed next to her tonight.

Not after it's become crystal fucking clear that I am still in love with Jessica Carrington.

Chapter Fifteen

JESS

Getting dressed after the massage is torture. My skin is flushed and tingling, the imprint of Nick's skin on mine still burning. I'm by myself in a locker room; taking my robe off shouldn't be arousing, and yet the feel of the fabric sliding over my skin is enough to send a shiver racing down my spine.

My head is as full of flurries as the blizzard still raging outside. I don't know what to think, much less what to feel after the last hour.

Nick regrets the ending, so he says. But I don't have much clarity as to what that actually means. The way he ended it, or the fact that he ended it at all? And what the hell am I supposed to do with that? Does that mean he wants to get back together? I flash back to what he said the other night at dinner, that his happy ending was destroyed. By whom? Because it sure as hell wasn't me.

And does it really matter? Will it make a difference if I discover Nick really does regret breaking up with me?

Will it make a difference if I find out he might want to explore getting back together?

Surely this shiver, zinging through every one of my veins and leaving my skin all tingly, can be chalked up to nothing short of horror at the thought of giving Nick and me another chance.

I peek around every doorway and every corner as I make my way back through the lobby. I've almost managed to make it to the elevators without running into Nick when I'm stopped by the only other person in this hotel I don't want to run into.

"Lauren!" I exclaim when she catches my elbow, pulling me to a halt in one of the alcoves of the lobby. "I'd say fancy running into you here, but since we're all trapped together, I guess it's par for the course." I wonder if I could manage to work any more clichés into my next sentence to really show off my stellar way with words.

"I'm glad I caught you, Jessica." She drops her hand from my elbow, since she literally caught me. "I was talking with Gina and Hannah this morning and they told me you and Nick might be writing a book together."

Oh god, please do not come out and directly ask me to fake date Nick Matthews. Because after the hour I just had, I might actually agree to the whole farcical plan, and I've been a romance reader for way longer than I've been a writer and I know the only outcome of a fake dating scheme is for it to become all too real.

Lauren hesitates for just a second, checking to make sure there's no one else around us. "I'm so excited to read what you guys come up with, I'm sure it's going to be absolutely fantastic."

"Oh." Well. Huh.

I try to identify the feeling building in the pit of my

stomach, but then I stop because I'm pretty sure it's disappointment. But that would mean I *wanted* to fake date Nick, and that, surely, is a ridiculous notion. There's no way I was sitting here, seriously waiting for one of the big deals at my publisher to ask me to fake date my ex-boyfriend.

Lauren is looking at me expectantly, like she needs more from me than a huff of breath.

And this is a woman with tons of power at my publisher, so I give it to her. "I'm super excited about it! Can't wait to dive in and really get to work!" So much for fewer clichés.

A genuine smile lights up her face. "I think I speak for everyone at SVP when I say we can't wait either. And I know I probably shouldn't even say this, but I did mean it, you know, when I said I'd noticed how Nick was looking at you. There might not be feelings there on your side anymore, but I'd be willing to bet he can't say the same." She pats my shoulder the way my mother would. "Hope you have a good holiday, I heard that the storm should be clearing up tonight. Hopefully we can all head home tomorrow, just in time for Christmas."

"Sounds amazing. Safe travels." I try to inject some cheer into my voice, but her assessment of Nick, combined with everything else that's happened in the past few days, well, it's just too much. The thought of our time here at the inn coming to an end tomorrow should bring a sense of relief, but as hard as I search for that particular emotion in the jumble that is my mind, I can't seem to find it. All I can parse out is uncertainty, and confusion, and a healthy dose of lingering lust.

I need clarity, and I need the truth.

So I march myself over to the elevator after a goodbye to Lauren. I stab at the button for our floor and continue my teenage-angst level stomping down the hallway to our door. I throw it open, expecting to find Nick lounging on the bed, or perched in the armchair, but of course the one time I actually want to see his face, he's nowhere to be found.

I pace around the room for a minute, attempting to get my thoughts in order. When it becomes clear my pouting isn't going to magically summon Nick from wherever the hell he is hiding out, I take out my computer and open our Google doc.

I find Nick's cursor almost immediately because it's right where I was headed to work out my sexual frustrations on the page—at the beginning of the sex scene. In each of our writing sessions we've had so far, we've ignored the spicy elephant in the room and skipped right over this section. I sort of assumed Nick would just leave me to write it, since it's much more in my wheelhouse than his.

Then again, the sex scenes in the books Nick has written since our split have garnered several chili peppers, but maybe the on-page magic he's written in the past can really be attributed to Gina's good editing.

I don't let myself imagine he's found himself another critique partner.

I consider starting up a conversation in the comments again, but instead, I just watch Nick's cursor, blinking away for a solid minute before words start to appear.

And I no longer wonder about who's responsible for Nick's sex scenes.

My mouth goes dry as I read in real time what Nick is writing. And there's something about knowing he's somewhere in this hotel, right this minute, with these kinds of images lingering in his mind. I'd like to say it has no effect on me, but I think it's clear that would be a big fat lie.

The words stop pouring across the page, and before I can think about why I shouldn't, I pick up right where he left off.

We take turns, going back and forth, giving and taking, and by the time we reach the climax of the scene—pun clearly intended—I'm breathless and a little bit sweaty, my heart pounding in my chest. Who knew writing could count as cardio?

I'm about to close my laptop, maybe go dive into one of the snow piles outside to cool my heated skin, but then Nick keeps typing.

He cups her cheek in his hand, perched over her, their chests pressed together so it feels as if their hearts beat as one. "I need you to know that I never stopped loving you. And if this is all you need from me, closure or one last time or a way to work out the sexual tension, if this is the last time I hold you in my arms, then I need you to know that I love you still. That I will love you always."

My heart stops in my chest.

Sure, these words are coming from our hero, but I can't help but wonder if they're also coming from Nick. We would be fools to deny the sexual tension between us—it's only been building since that first moment backstage, when just a single brush of his skin on mine sent my goose bumps into overdrive.

But is there something deeper here? Can there be something more?

Nick has only been back in my life less than a week—two if we want to count the week of DMing—but the impact is already undeniable. From the way his banter stoked the creative part of my brain that was dormant for months to the way a simple brush of his skin against mine during our stupid massage was more arousing than all the foreplay of my last three one-night stands combined. I would be an idiot to forget how he hurt me, but am I also an idiot if I don't fully explore this? Even if it turns out to be nothing?

Part of me wants to reach out to Alyssa and Kennedy, call in some backup, but the bigger part of me is too afraid of what they might say. I feel like that should act as a warning of some sort, but I choose to ignore it.

Besides, time is of the essence here. Something tells me that once we leave this inn, once we lose this forced proximity, it will be too easy to walk away and never look back. Never get the answers I really need.

I slam my laptop shut before I call down to room service, ordering dinner and a bottle of wine. I travel down the hallway to the ice machine, filling the bucket so we have it on hand for later. I notice the bottle of whiskey has been cracked, but there's still plenty left, more than enough for my needs.

I take a quick shower and put on some makeup. I've

been wearing the same outfit for three days now, and my wardrobe options are limited. My underwear rotation means I'm back in the red lace thong and bra, thank god. I could put my red dress from the party back on, but I want to be comfortable, and nothing about sitting in skintight fabric is comfortable. So I slide into my jeans and steal a T-shirt from Nick's bag. The cotton is soft on my skin, and it smells like him. I indulge in a whiff because there's no one around to see me.

And then, when I'm fully ready, I take out my phone and text him. It's been so long since I sent him a text that our old messages have disappeared, lost to the years of phone upgrades.

ME: Can you come up to the room? I think we need to talk.

It doesn't take him more than a second to answer me.

NICK: Be right there.

I take a few steadying breaths. Though I'm not sure I'll ever be truly ready for this. I don't even know what I want to say to him, I just know that that elusive closure seems to be dangling right in front of me and this is my way of reaching out and grabbing it.

When the door to the room opens a minute later, I'm sitting in the armchair. The room service has been delivered, the extremely nice and patient employee helped me arrange the rolly little table in between the bed and armchair so we can both sit and pretend like we're grown-ups having a real meal together.

Nick's eyebrows shoot to the top of his forehead as he takes in the scene. "What's all this?"

I gesture for him to take a seat. "I figured it was time we cut the bullshit and have a real conversation."

His eyebrows creep up even farther. "Should I be scared right now? Why do I feel a sense of foreboding overcoming me?"

"Haha. I took the liberty of ordering dinner." I wave my hands over the table like Vanna White.

"If this is my Christmas present, I feel like I should let you know I didn't get you anything." Nick hesitates for a second more before awkwardly sliding onto the bed and tucking his long legs under the tiny table.

I pick up my glass of wine and hold it up. "Cheers."

Nick clinks his glass against mine. "What exactly are we toasting to?"

"How about an evening of honesty?" I look him right in the eyes as I sip my wine. I can't afford seven years of bad sex, and I'm not taking any chances.

Nick's brow furrows and there's more than a hint of trepidation in his eyes. "Can I at least enjoy my dinner first?"

"I suppose." I dig into the pasta dish sitting in front of me. It's not bad, considering we've been eating from the same restaurant for days in a row.

"I stopped by the front desk on my way up and they let me know the storm is supposed to pass tonight. You should be able to head home tomorrow." Nick takes a bite of his own pasta and lets out a little groan of appreciation.

I swallow thickly before responding because that groan sounded a lot like arousal, and we are not going there right now. "Yeah, I ran into Lauren in the lobby a little bit ago and she mentioned that."

"I'm sure you're excited to be getting out of here."

I nod, though it feels like a lie. "You too, I'm sure."

"I booked my room through the twenty-sixth, so I'll be sticking around no matter what." He downs a long swallow of wine. "Are you going to your parents' house for Christmas?"

I shake my head. "It's a travel year for them."

Ever since that first Christmas Nick and I spent together, when I encouraged my parents to hit the road for the purely selfish reason of wanting to be alone with my new boyfriend, my parents have alternated between holidays at home with me and holidays traveling around the world. Usually the years when they're not home, I go to Alyssa's or Kennedy's, or one or both of them come to me. But this year, it seems I'll be all on my own.

I had been looking forward to it, honestly. But now the thought of waking up alone on Christmas sounds nothing short of awful.

"How are they doing?"

"They're great. Out there living their best retirement lives." My parents loved Nick, and though they respect me enough to never ask about him, I know for a fact my mom has read every single one of his books and follows him on Instagram.

"Please give them my best."

"I will." The outcome of this dinner will determine whether or not I do. I finish the rest of my wine. "How is your family doing?"

Nick refills my glass before answering. "They're fine."

He doesn't elaborate, and I don't push. I only met Nick's parents once in the three years we were together. They're not bad people, and as far as I can tell, Nick had a perfectly pleasant childhood. But he doesn't have much in common with his family, and once he moved to New York for college, none of them seemed too invested in staying in contact. I don't think they ever got over him leaving Ohio and choosing not to join the family business. It wasn't until he reached out to them with news of his upcoming six-figure book deal that they seemed to start to take him seriously, like his success suddenly made him worthwhile in their eyes. It always made me sad to think about when Nick and I were dating, but I think he's okay with where their relationship stands, so I learned to leave it alone. I wonder if and how things have changed as he's become more and more of a household name.

Nick clears his throat, drawing my attention to the troubled look in his hazel eyes. "I hope nothing that happened today, during the massage . . . or after, made you uncomfortable. That's the last thing I would want."

"I know. And I wasn't uncomfortable." Unless by uncomfortable, you mean uncomfortably aroused, that is. "This week sure has thrown a lot at us. I think we're handling it as best we could."

"Things haven't exactly gone to plan, but I can't say I'm sorry at how they've turned out." He swirls the wine in his glass.

"How do you mean?"

"I mean, it's been really good to see you again, Jess." His voice is soft, layered with emotions. "I don't think I realized how much I missed you until I saw you backstage."

"That was probably mostly the dress," I quip, needing to brush off the heaviness of his sentiment.

The corner of his mouth quirks up in what used to be my favorite half smile. "It sure as fuck didn't hurt."

My cheeks heat, and I know from experience they're turning the color of the red wine left in my glass. I want to return his sentiment, about missing him, because I realize, sitting here with him and having a normal conversation, that it's true. I have missed him. But I don't know if I'm ready to admit it.

I divide the small amount of wine remaining in the bottle between each of our glasses. "You know how you always used to tell me that I rely too much on the miscommunication trope in my books?"

He frowns a little, confused about the shift in topic, but then he nods. "And you used to tell me that in real life, couples not being able to communicate was one of the biggest relationship struggles people have."

"I stand by that." I take in a deep breath. "But tonight, I want us to do better."

Nick pushes his plate away, though he's only eaten half of his pasta. I don't think I can eat another bite either. I swig the last of my wine, and Nick does the same. We stack up our dishes and maneuver the table out into the hallway. I hang the Do Not Disturb sign on the knob before letting the door click shut behind me.

Nick resumes his position on the bed. Before I sink back into the armchair, I put a few ice cubes into two glasses and pour each of us a decent-sized slug of whiskey.

When I hand Nick his glass, our fingers brush and I experience one of those moments I've only written about, when a spark jumps between us.

"Here's what I propose." I settle into the armchair and

wish this room were bigger so there could be a little more breathing room separating us. "We take turns asking questions. Honest answers only. If you don't want to answer, you drink."

He studies the caramel-colored liquid in his glass. "This seems like a dangerous game, Jess."

I shrug. "Only if you aren't willing to tell the truth."

He sighs, and I watch the debate play out over his face. "Okay. But I reserve the right to put a stop to this at any point if things get out of hand."

I roll my eyes. "Fine. I'll even be generous and let you go first."

His head tilts to the side as he thinks. He always used to do that when he was writing and the familiar motion warms something in my already wine-warmed chest. "What's your favorite book you've written?"

"Hmm. I love them all, obviously. But I think *With a Twist* is my favorite. There's nothing like your first, I suppose."

Nick nods, but I get the feeling he isn't even really listening to my response. I can tell by the way his eyes pinch at the corners that he's already stressed about what I'm going to ask him. And I'd be lying if I said that didn't send a little thrill through me.

"My turn." I smile at him, going for warm and friendly so he'll feel at ease before I throw down the gauntlet. "Are you still in love with me?"

Chapter Sixteen

NICK

I t's a good thing I haven't yet sampled the whiskey because I'd be choking on it. Or spitting it out like some sitcom character.

"Jesus, Jess. Not going to ease me in, are you?" I realize the innuendo the moment the words are out of my mouth.

She raises one eyebrow. "You know that's not how I like it."

She sounds so bold, so confident, but her flushed cheeks give her away.

I sip from my glass while I formulate my thoughts.

Jess's eyes fill with disappointment.

"I'm not not answering, I just need a drink before I do." I let the liquor burn a path down my chest and warm my belly. But I'm not sure even half a bottle of whiskey would be enough to give me the courage to say what I know I need to.

"Take as long as you need," she says softly.

My eyes meet hers, and there's no denying the truth. "Of course I'm still in love with you, Jess." I think we've both known since I saw her backstage, maybe even since I sent her that first DM, and yet, it feels like some kind of relief to say it out loud. "How could I not be?"

She blinks in surprise before giving me a wry smile. "Is that your next question?"

I chuckle, but there's no real humor in it. "No, it's not. I . . ." I want to say more, give her more, but she stops me with a shake of her head.

"All you owe me is one answer, Nick. You don't need to explain. Your turn for a question." She holds her glass up to her lips, but doesn't drink, a teasing glint in her eyes.

I don't know how she can be so casual, so calm, when I just laid my whole heart bare, but something tells me she knew the answer to her question before I gave it. She always has been able to see right through me. "What accomplishment are you most proud of?"

Her head tilts to the side as she thinks, lowering the glass to rest on the arm of the chair. "Probably making it through my second book. I always thought authors were exaggerating about the sophomore slump, but it hit me hard. I hated writing that book, but now looking back on it, I'm so proud of how it came out."

This chuckle is laced with real humor. "I felt the exact same way. I thought my second book might kill me."

Of course, for both of us, our second books were the first books we'd written without each other. I'd always known how much I relied on Jess's feedback and critiques, but it became wholly evident how much she contributed to my process when I sat down to write without her by my side.

"What's something still left on your bucket list?" She surprises me with her change in direction. She came out of the gate hot, and I'm shocked she's now veering toward easier topics.

Still, I bring my glass to my lips and drink. I already admitted I'm still in love with her, and the only things left on my bucket list involve finding a partner and settling down. Marriage and maybe a kid one day. I can't lay that out there without something in return from her first.

"Really? You won't answer that one?"

I shrug and smile, trying to keep things light and mysterious and likely failing miserably at both. "What's something still left on your bucket list?" I throw the easy question back at her.

She rolls her eyes at my cheating. "Everything. Most of us haven't already hit every list and seen our books made into blockbuster movies. I've hardly accomplished anything."

I shake my head. "That's not true, Jess. When we first met, your goal was to get an agent and get published and write more books and have fans make art of your characters, all things you've been able to check off your list."

She takes a swig from her drink even though there's no question on the table. "How do you know I've had fans make art of my characters?"

This time it's my cheeks heating, because of course I check her Instagram. Pretty religiously, though I'm not going to admit that to her. "My point is, it's easy to keep moving the goalposts, but it's important to remember that the you from ten years ago would be so thrilled to see where you are now."

"I suppose." She swirls her glass around, the ice clinking merrily. "Do you miss being in a relationship?"

"With you? Yes." I meet her gaze head on. "Do you miss being in a relationship with me?"

She downs the rest of the whiskey in her glass without a word.

I drink too, in solidarity, before standing up and topping us both off. I purse my lips together so I don't let my excitement show, because if the answer was no, she would have just said so.

She misses me.

It's something, at least.

Jess moves us back to safer topics, her next couple of questions lightly inquiring about my process and if I have any ideas for what to work on next. I return the favor. The questions seem surface level and easy, but I love the way she lights up when she's talking about her writing, when she talks about meeting readers and mentoring newer authors.

We both continue to sip from our drinks, even though we're answering each question the other poses. The whiskey and the wine and sitting across from Jess all melt together in my chest, warming me from the inside out. I could go traipsing through the blizzard outside right now and probably not feel a thing.

Until Jess pivots back into dangerous territory, sending an uncomfortable chill through me. "Do you think you'll ever write a book with a happy ending?"

I'm tempted to drink and stave off the question. It's one that's posed to me fairly often, though not as much now as it was in the beginning of my career. My brand is well established at this point, and I think a lot of my fans would probably be disappointed with a happy ending in a Nick

Matthews book. But it was never what I set out to write, and I know this breaking of the genre's foremost rule has always kept me sidelined in the romance community. In terms of our careers, it's the one thing Jess has that I don't—a spot in the community we both love.

So I give her an honest answer. "I don't know."

She gives me a pointed look. "That's a cop-out."

"It's the truth. I'm not opposed to happy endings, I can't say with certainty I'll never write one, but I can't promise I will either. I don't know how to write something that seems so impossible."

She tosses back another sip of whiskey. "And yet, I manage to write them just fine, and I'm the one who had my heart broken."

I run my thumb along the rim of my glass, studying the motion so I don't have to look at her. "I know it doesn't seem like it, but it broke my heart too, Jess."

"Then why did you do it?"

I've been waiting for that. The one question I can't answer, not even when I ask it of myself. "I think it's my turn to ask a question."

"Fine then. Go ahead."

"Are you still attracted to me?" I know it's a question I shouldn't be asking, but it's the best way I can think of to divert her. The chemistry between us was always palpable, and nothing about that has changed. This might be the only way to steer her off course. "Do you ever think about me when you, you know . . ."

Her cheeks flush, but she's not going down without a fight. She leans forward in her chair. "Do I think about you when I what? Have sex with someone else?"

I shut my eyes against that image. "No. Do you ever think about me when you touch yourself, Jess?"

She waits for me to open my eyes and meet her gaze before she slowly brings her glass up to her lips. Her tongue darts out, licking a stray drop of liquor from the rim. Then she drinks.

I grin in triumph.

Her eyes narrow. "Do you ever think about me when you touch yourself?"

I raise my glass but don't sip. "All the fucking time."

Her breath catches in her chest. "Jesus, Nick," she mumbles.

I love seeing her flustered, and so I keep pushing. "Of all the times we slept together, which was the best for you? I know they were all good, of course, but which time stands out the most?"

For a second, I think she won't answer, but I catch the moment when she realizes I have the upper hand. It plays across her face. And I see the moment when she decides to fight back. Which is exactly what I want. Because if she asks me again why I broke up with her, I might actually tell her.

She rests her elbows on her knees, the glass of whiskey cupped in her hands. The move makes it easy for me to see down the deep vee of her shirt. My shirt. I always loved seeing her wear my clothes, and now, with the outline of her lacy red bra visible, well, I shift in my seat a little, the tightness of my jeans becoming uncomfortable.

"There were quite a few. But I think my favorite one was that one time at my parents' house."

I suck in a breath. Our second Christmas. The only holiday we ever spent with her parents. The only time I've ever had sex with someone in their parents' house. I'd been against it from the start, but when Jess had locked that door behind us and stripped off her top, I'd been a goner. I'd had to cover her mouth to keep her from screaming the whole house awake.

I adjust my position again, knowing that if she looks, she'll be able to see how much one single memory is affecting me.

"Tell me about your favorite time, Nick." Her voice has dropped, and her smile is knowing. Her eyes glance down to my pants, but I cover myself with my almost-empty glass. That only makes her smile wider.

"Every time with you was incredible, Jess. But that first Christmas, you were wearing a lacy red bra a lot like the one you are not-so-subtly trying to get me to look at right now. You dropped to your knees in the middle of the living room and took me in your mouth. It was fucking perfect." I let my gaze linger on the hint of scarlet lace peeking out of her shirt.

The flush from her cheeks spreads down to her chest, and when I finally tear my eyes away, I see her eyes are almost black in the low lighting of the room.

She sets her whiskey glass on the side table next to the chair. "What would you do to me, right now, if I stripped off this shirt and told you to make me come? How would you touch me, Nick?"

My mouth goes dry. That took an unexpected turn. I set down my own glass. "Jess, I don't know if this is a good idea. I was just teasing, trying to get a rise out of you."

Her eyes drift down to my crotch. "I seem to have succeeded in getting a rise out of you."

I choke on a laugh. "You usually do."

She sits back in the chair and stares me down. "Are you going to answer?"

I wipe my hands on my thighs. "We've been drinking. I'm not going to touch you while you're drunk."

"I'm not drunk. And I don't want you to touch me. I want you to talk to me." She fingers the hem of her shirt like she's thinking about removing it.

"Isn't it my turn to ask the question?"

She shrugs. "So ask."

"What's the best book you've read lately?"

She reaches for her glass and swallows the last sip of whiskey. "My turn. What would you do to me to make me come?"

Chapter Seventeen

JESS

Fuck me, I'm going to regret this.

Somewhere between the wine and the whiskey and the even more intoxicating sound of Nick's voice, I completely lost the plot. This was supposed to be about closure, putting the final nail in the coffin of a relationship that's been haunting me for years.

Instead, I'm too close to a man I'm still deadly attracted to. His dick is hard, my panties are wet, and I'm practically daring him to talk dirty to me.

Note to self: No more whiskey. Like ever.

Nick hesitates for so long I start to think he's going to refuse to answer. That would be the smart thing to do.

Apparently, we're both idiots.

Nick's voice is low and rumbly, and when he begins to speak, I have to shake off a shiver. "If you took off that shirt right now, Jess, I think at first I would have to just sit here and look at you."

Goddamn it. Why is that the hottest thing he could possibly say?

"You're gorgeous, always, but when you're aroused,

Jess. I can barely stand it. Your chest flushes the same bright red as your cheeks. Even your nipples flush, a perfect rosy pink. I'd lick along the edge of that lace before letting my tongue trail down. I want to tease you, torture you a bit"—he gives me a wicked grin—"and I want to take my time. It's been so long, and I've missed the feel of your soft skin under my lips."

Holy hell. I am the stupidest person alive because this is so not what I expected, and I am not prepared. Nick already demonstrated earlier today just how deftly he can write a sex scene, why didn't I realize those talents would extend to narrating? We're only a few sentences in and my nipples are hard as diamonds.

"Do you want me to stop?"

I know I should say yes.

Instead, I shake my head.

He takes a deep breath. "Once you're writhing underneath me, grinding against me and searching for relief, I would kiss my way down your stomach, unbuttoning your jeans, pulling them down just enough so I could lick along the dip of your hip bone."

Of course he remembers my secret sensitive spot, the one no man since him has even come close to discovering.

"Are you wearing the red lace panties, Jess?"

I nod, unsure what might come spilling out of me if I open my mouth. I'd probably beg him to stop talking and fuck me already, and we can't have that.

He lets out a little groan and his hand moves to his crotch, tugging at his jeans. I can see the outline of him through the fabric and I have to look away so I don't fling myself across the room and onto his lap.

"I'd kiss you through the lace of your panties, see how ready you are for me."

So ready. I'm so fucking ready.

"Dammit, Jess, you can't say shit like that right now."

Oops.

Nick rises from the bed and strides to the far corner of the room, putting the maximum amount of space between us. It breaks some kind of trance, the spell both of us have been under.

"I'm sorry," I say after a weighted silence. "I should never have asked that of you. You can stop."

"I don't want to stop," he grumbles. "I just . . ." He scrubs a hand over his face. "This was a bad idea. You don't really want me. Not the way I want you. This can only end with more hurt feelings, and there's been enough of those already."

"You're right." I don't clarify as to what he's right about, because I'm not totally sure myself, other than one of us is likely to get hurt if we continue down this path.

"I'm going to take a cold shower. And then I'll sleep on the floor tonight."

I nod, though I can think of nothing I want less. I stay frozen in the chair.

Nick brushes by me on the way to the bathroom. He pauses in front of me, then drops a kiss on my forehead. "I wish I could tell you everything, Jess, but if you only take away one thing from this week, I hope it's that I never stopped loving you. And I never will."

Nick has made it clear he has no intention of explaining what went wrong between us five years ago. But I'm honestly starting to not really care.

Of course, that could be the whiskey talking. And my libido.

But he's been so open about everything else. I mean, the man straight up told me he's still in love with me. I don't know that I can say I feel the same, but I'm a hell of a lot less opposed to the idea than I was just a week ago. Maybe it's time to open myself up to the possibility of us, the possibility that it doesn't really matter what happened the first time.

Maybe the only thing that matters now is what happens tonight, and tomorrow, and the day after that. A possible future.

Chapter Eighteen

NICK

The cold shower doesn't do much to ease my mind. Still, I stand under the pounding chilled water for longer than I should, hoping for even a hint of clarification of what to do next. I laid it all out there, told her exactly how I feel, and even though I can't give her the full story or the answers she really wants, she knows I'm still in love with her.

When I've delayed the inevitable for as long as possible, I pull on my flannel pajama pants and head back into the room. I don't look at her as she practically dives into the bathroom, shutting the door firmly behind her.

Jess doesn't take nearly as long as I did in the shower, and when I hear the water shut off, I stand up. I've got a pillow and a bundle of blankets in my arms when the door opens, letting out a cloud of steam.

She's wearing the shirt I gave her that first night to sleep in. And since the shirt is white, it becomes immediately clear that she's not wearing anything underneath except those motherfucking lacy red panties.

This woman is going to be the death of me.

She closes the distance between us and takes the pillow and blankets from me, tossing them back on the bed. "I don't want you to sleep on the floor."

"I appreciate it, Jess, but this is more for me than for you. I can't lie there next to you and pretend like the past few hours haven't happened."

She slips her hand into mine. "I don't want you to."

My fingers tighten around hers almost instinctively. "We're still too buzzed to be making any kind of major decisions. I'm not going to sleep with you tonight if there's even a chance you might regret it in the morning." That might be the thing that finally does me in.

"We don't have to do anything, Nick. I just want to wake up next to you."

She might as well have punched me in the chest because it takes a second before I'm able to breathe.

"What are you really saying, Jess?"

She shrugs, the motion causing her shirt to slip off her shoulder. "I'm saying we don't have to make any major decisions tonight, but I'm also saying I can't stomach the thought of you sleeping on the floor."

"Because it might strain my old-man back?"

"Because I would rather have you next to me."

I close my eyes for a brief moment, hoping it might stave off the headache I can feel building at my temples. I'm not sure if it's from the alcohol or the blue balls or the way her words are twisting up my brain, but I need it to go away. "Okay." I cave because of course I do. I always do when it comes to her.

We both settle into our assigned sides of the bed, keeping a fair amount of distance between us, but forgoing the pillow barrier. I take a long swig of water and turn out my light, burrowing under the covers and leaving my back to her. I have my limits, and tonight, mine are not looking at her hair spilling across the pillow, or the small smile that always tugs on her lips when she's sleeping, like she's having the most pleasant of dreams.

"Good night, Nick," she whispers. Her light clicks off and the room falls into darkness.

"Good night, Jess." I close my eyes, even though I know sleep isn't going to find me tonight. It's easier to let the darkness swallow me from the inside out.

The red numbers of the hotel alarm clock inform me it's just after three in the morning when my eyes pop back open, my bladder protesting for relief, my mouth dry.

I slip out of bed and pad as quietly as possible to the bathroom, where I relieve myself before sticking my mouth under the tap and drinking for a solid two minutes. I swig some mouthwash and swallow some aspirin and feel markedly better.

Tiptoeing back to my side of the bed, I climb in between the sheets as slowly as possible, hoping not to jostle Jess out of her sleep. But her eyes flutter open and she smiles at me sleepily. I wait for the realization to overtake her, for her to remember just where we are and why.

But her smile doesn't fade.

In fact, as I nestle back under the covers, she scoots over to my side of the bed, tucking herself into the crook of my arm. My hand immediately finds its way into her hair, scratching her scalp and tugging gently on the roots, the way she always liked.

She groans, burrowing closer into my chest. Her fingers trace light circles on the bare skin of my stomach, and never has a more innocent touch been so arousing.

"How are you feeling?" My voice is husky, made more so by the torture her fingers are delivering to my skin.

"I feel fine." She tilts her chin up to look me in the eye. "I told you I wasn't drunk, you know."

"I know, and I believed you, but I woke up with a sore head."

She props her chin on my chest. "I guess I just hold my liquor better than you. Though I do need to use the bathroom."

She scoots out of bed and flits into the restroom, returning a minute later and sliding right back into my embrace.

I let out the breath I'd been holding in since she got up, unsure if her escaping the bed was going to break some kind of spell.

She sighs, her breath tickling my chest. "I forgot how good you are at cuddling."

My fingers resume their trail through the strands of her hair. "It is one of my better traits."

We sit in silence for a moment, but it's comfortable, and peaceful.

"I don't really know what we're doing here, Nick." Her voice is so soft I barely hear her, and probably wouldn't if she weren't so close.

"I don't either, but you're in control here. This can be

whatever you want it to be. Or whatever you don't want it to be." My hold on her tightens without me having to think about it.

"I want you," she whispers, an admission that could easily be lost in the night.

I have to swallow the lump in my throat. "I want you too."

"Even if it's only for tonight?"

I slam my eyes closed, letting my senses breathe her in. Tomorrow morning the roads will be cleared, and Jess will go home. We can very easily finish writing this book from the comfort of our own separate homes. It will be months before we have to see each other in person again. If she wants to walk out of this room in the morning without a look back, there won't be anything I can do to stop her.

One last time with the love of my life.

Even if there's a solid chance that having her just to lose her might actually kill me.

But I can deny this woman nothing. And I don't want to deny her this. I want her—I need her—no matter what happens next.

I move my hand from her hair to the curve of her jaw, running my thumb along the smooth skin of her cheek. "I'm here for whatever the rest of the night brings us, Jess. Whatever you want from me, I'm here to give it. Willingly." I tip her chin up, but I wait for her to close the distance between us.

She studies me for a long second first, her deep brown eyes full of questions, like mine might hold all the answers.

The first brush of her lips against mine is as fleeting as a snowflake landing on your eyelashes and melting away a second later.

The second press of her lips against mine absolutely wrecks me, destroys me, breaks me, and heals me all in one go.

Chapter Nineteen

JESS

Oh god. This is either the best or worst decision I've ever made in my entire life. Best because, holy shit, I forgot how good Nick Matthews is at kissing. Worst because, holy shit, I forgot how good Nick Matthews is at kissing.

How am I going to wake up in the morning—in just a few hours from now—and pretend like he hasn't just kissed me like the world is ending? Thank god I'm already lying down, because I know my knees wouldn't be able to support me as Nick's lips move over mine, as he sucks my bottom lip in between his, letting his teeth nibble along the delicate skin before his tongue tangles with mine. The kiss is slow and languid, and heat pools in my belly and, fuck, I don't think I've ever wanted anyone as much as I want him in this moment.

I can't stop touching him, can't stop my hands from roaming over every inch of his skin. My hands trail up the bare expanse of his chest, down over the ridges of his abs, around to the solid muscles of his back. He shifts his weight, his hips pressing my legs open as his mouth continues to devour mine.

When he breaks the kiss, it's only to let his mouth move along the line of my jaw, down my neck. His teeth graze the place where my shoulder and neck meet.

"More," I demand, twining my legs with his, pulling him down on top of me. The weight of him over me is delicious and warm and comforting, and when the hard length of him presses against my core, I groan.

Nick heeds my request, marking me with his teeth and soothing the skin with a brush of his tongue. He puts the slightest bit of space between us and his pupils widen, the hazel of his eyes almost completely obstructed. "Jesus, Jess." He rolls his hips, slow enough that I can feel every inch of him, waiting for me.

My hand skirts down his stomach and I palm him through the fabric of his pajama pants. This time he's the one letting out the unholy groan, the sound of it hitting me right in my core.

He takes my hand in his, lacing our fingers together and bringing our joined hands over my head. "It's going to be hard enough for me to last without your hands all over me."

I squeeze his hand and shift my hips up to meet his. "I want to touch you, Nick."

"I promise I'll let you do whatever you want to me, but you've got to let me take my time with you first." He trails a single finger along the exposed edge of my collarbone and somehow this simple touch is the hottest thing I've ever felt.

"Fine," I sigh, like he's really putting me out with all the foreplay.

He grins, kissing the smirk right off my face. Eventually his mouth moves down once again, licking along the neckline of his shirt. My nipples are peaked and the fabric is thin, and when his mouth descends, my back arches off the bed, reaching for him.

His hands fist in the hem of the shirt and he drags it slowly up, baring my panties and then the skin of my belly. His lips follow the shirt as it continues upward. He licks at the undersides of my breasts before finally baring me to the chilly air. I take that as permission to yank the damn shirt over my head.

Nick shifts his weight, pulling himself away from me and resting on his knees. His eyes rove over me, and for half a second I wonder if he's disappointed in what he sees. It's been a few years and I'm sure my body has changed.

"Why did you stop?"

"Just a pause. I wanted to—"

"Do not give me some cheesy line from one of your books like you had to stop and drink me in because you can't believe how beautiful my skin looks in the moonlight."

He drags his fingers from my belly button up to the swell of my chest. "Your skin does look beautiful in the moonlight." His fingers lock around one nipple, pinching with just enough pressure, while his tongue swipes at the other. "And I do want to drink you in, Jess. I want to kiss every part of you, see what still makes you squirm and what makes you sigh." He sucks the bud into his mouth, his teeth grazing the sensitive skin.

My fingers dig into his hair, pulling him closer, silently

begging him for more. He releases me before I want him to, but then his mouth is on the move again and his tongue is tracing the line of my hip bone.

And there's his sought-after sigh. He remembered my favorite spot.

"Of course I remembered," he whispers and I'm not sure if I voiced my thoughts out loud or if he just knows me well enough by now to hear them anyway.

My eyes flutter closed because I'm too overwhelmed with sensations to focus, and Nick is doing things to my body that no one else ever has and dammit, I missed this. I missed him.

And it's so good. Maybe it's too good. Maybe this was a terrible idea.

My whole body tenses as I wonder if we're making a huge fucking mistake.

Nick pauses his ministrations, bringing his hand up to cup my cheek. "Hey. You okay?"

I nod, keeping my eyes clenched firmly shut.

"Jessica. Look at me and tell me that you're really okay." His weight shifts off of me and I miss the warmth and comfort of him instantly.

I push down the threat of tears because I am not going to do that right now. I open my eyes and immediately find his, the hazel tinged with worry. "I'm okay."

He tucks a strand of hair behind my ear. "What's going on in that gorgeous head of yours?"

I reach for him, my hand finding a place on his chest. His heart beats furiously under my palm, and I let the rhythm of it ground me. "This is just a lot, you know? I don't think I realized how much I missed you until this very moment."

"I'm right here. And I'll be here as long as you want me to be. Okay?"

I look for the catch, the deception or the empty promise hidden in his pretty words. But there isn't one. All I see in Nick's eyes is honesty, and hope, and maybe even a little bit of love.

"Okay." I bring his mouth down to mine, but he keeps the kiss short.

He settles onto his back, tucking me into his chest in the same cuddle position we were in earlier.

"What are you doing?" I shift onto my side so I can look at him easier.

"If you're having any qualms, we're not doing this, Jess."

I roll my eyes. "I'm not having qualms, Nick, I was having emotions. You are not going to get me this worked up and then not get me off. That's just rude."

He chuckles, the nerve of him. "How worked up are you?"

I take his hand and guide it in between my legs. I'm still wearing my fancy red underwear, but I know my wetness has soaked through the fabric. He cups me, and I roll my hips so the heel of his palm presses down on my clit.

"Jesus, Jess, you're so wet."

I'm not sure why he seems surprised by this information, given the delectable torture his mouth was engaged in just a few minutes ago. "What are you going to do about it?"

His hesitation lasts for less than a second. "Take off your panties."

The command leaves me a little breathless, but I don't hesitate to obey. My eyes trail down to the bulge in his pants and it twitches as I return to his side, fully bared to him.

"Come here." Nick takes my hips in his hands and guides me, positions me so my knees are on either side of his head.

I suck in a breath.

This is new.

It's something I've written about in my books, but never actually tried myself. I'm sure Nick would have been up for it, but I was always too self-conscious to ask. I don't often live out my fantasies on the page, but I'll make an exception for this.

"Have you read my books, Nick Matthews?"

He grins up at me, pulling me closer to his waiting mouth. "Maybe." He leans up, running the tip of his tongue through my center. "I always wanted to try this with you, you know."

I settle myself over him, finding a comfortable position, gasping as Nick's tongue slides over my clit. "Why didn't you say anything?"

He pulls away, and I groan at the loss. "I guess I always thought we would have plenty of time."

He doesn't give me a chance to respond, tugging my hips down to him. His mouth—always so skilled—works over me, licking, sucking, until I'm writhing over him. I have to grab on to the headboard just to keep myself upright. Nick's hands grab my ass, dragging me closer as he devours me.

The orgasm doesn't build, it barrels into me, almost knocking me over. My muscles tighten and lock, and the cry that escapes me is guttural. I don't know how I manage to keep myself upright as the waves of release threaten to pull me under. But Nick keeps a tight hold on me, wringing every single drop of pleasure from me before placing a single light kiss on my clit.

I hover over him for a second, unsure I can make any of my limbs work. "Holy shit."

He grins proudly. He's earned it. "Good?"

"If your goal was to ruin me for other partners, I'd say mission accomplished."

He wraps his arms around me and flips me over in one slick move. "Good."

"Why do you still have pants on?"

He laughs and shimmies out of them, giving me my first good look at him in five years. Nick always had a perfect cock, and I'm happy to report he still does.

He hops out of bed and disappears into the bathroom, coming back with a condom in hand.

"May I?" I take the packet from him, stroking him a few times before ripping open the condom and rolling it over him.

"You sure about this?" There's so much self-doubt layered in his question it breaks my heart a little.

"So sure. The most sure." I cup his cheek in my hand. He hasn't shaved in the days since we've been stuck here and his stubble scratches at my palm.

He turns his head, kissing my palm before pushing into me, slowly. So slowly I think I might die. But then he's fully seated inside of me, his forehead pressed against mine.

I lean up, reaching for his lips, and his kiss is just as slow as his thrusts. I can still taste myself on him, and despite the frantic, deliciously dirty act that just got me off, Nick fucks me like he never wants it to end. Like he wants to be buried inside of me forever, like he never wants us to part.

He fucks me like he still loves me.

And somewhere in between—in the moment when his hand grips my hip to pull me closer, in the moment my fingers twine into the hair at the nape of his neck, in the moment his fingers reach between us to make sure I find my pleasure before his rushes through him—somewhere in there, I realize I still love him too.

Chapter Twenty

NICK

'm not sure what time it is when I finally manage to pry my eyes open, thanks to the gift of hotel-issue blackout curtains, but given the fact that I actually feel somewhat rested, it has to be at least late morning, if not early afternoon.

After the best sex of my life, Jess and I stayed up talking and kissing and cuddling, and yes, giving each other several more orgasms before we finally fell asleep. It had to be early this morning, so who knows what time it might be now.

Which means the roads have been cleared, and Jess is now free to go home.

I look down at her, her gorgeous face peaceful and content, resting on my chest. I always hated sleep cuddling, could never make myself actually fall asleep with another person so intertwined in my space. But Jess converted me. So many things I found untenable before she came along suddenly became manageable with her.

After last night and this morning, there are no more

doubts left in my mind. Jessica Carrington is the woman I'm meant to be with. The only thing left to do now is bare it all. Tell her the truth, the full truth, and hope she can find it in her heart to forgive me, that somehow, after all these years, she is willing to give me another chance.

I'm not sure I can survive losing her again.

But for now, she's here, wrapped in my arms. Neither of us bothered to put our pajamas back on and the feel of her soft skin against mine is nothing short of heavenly. I brush back a loose lock of her chocolate-brown hair, twining the silky strand around my finger.

She stirs, her bare legs tangled with mine, the brush of her thigh against my cock stirring me in turn.

My hand freezes, still tangled in her hair. I made sure to check in with her frequently throughout the night's actions, but that doesn't mean she won't wake up this morning and regret everything. I wait for her eyes to open, for her to meet my gaze.

A soft smile spreads across her lips, still swollen from our kisses. "Good morning."

I can't stop the grin on my own face. "Good morning. Though I think there's a pretty good chance we're firmly in afternoon territory now."

She sighs and snuggles deeper into my chest. "I don't really care what time it is as long as the coffee cart is still open and serving peppermint mochas."

"Some things never change, I see."

Her fingers begin a maddening trail, tracing over the lines of my stomach. "Some things change quite a lot."

"Jess . . . I want you to know that my feelings for you, they never changed. I never stopped loving you."

She props her chin on my chest. "You made that quite clear last night."

I search for the deeper meaning, the hidden messages in her words, but her eyes give away nothing. "I want to tell you everything. Explain what really happened. If you want to hear, that is. If not, and last night was just some kind of closure you needed to get to move on, well, then I understand." Letting her go will be like removing my heart from my chest and shipping it off to the North Pole, but something tells me to hold back a little on the dramatics.

"I want to hear what you have to say," she says quietly, pressing her lips to my chest. "I don't know what last night was yet, but it certainly didn't feel like closure."

My heart swells three sizes, but I can't let myself jump too far ahead. I'm scared to say anything else, worried I'll frighten her away, so I take her chin in my hand and lean down to meet her for a kiss.

Jess slips out of the bed first, heading into the bathroom and shutting the door behind her. The sound of the water running doesn't drown out the Mariah Carey Christmas song she hums, and when she emerges, there's a grin etched on her face. She's pulled her hair back into a bun and left her face bare, but I have to latch on to the sheets to keep me in place when I see she's wearing just her jeans and that blasted lacy red bra.

She heads over to the closet, where I unpacked and hung up all my clothes on our first day here. She rifles through my things, finally selecting a soft gray hoodie, which she tugs over her head. And somehow she looks even better in my sweatshirt than she did in her lingerie.

I groan and flop back onto the pillows, my eyes glued to

the ceiling. "You know how much I love seeing you in my clothes, Jess."

"Just so you know, you're never getting this sweatshirt back."

"Keep it. I'll only end up sleeping with it to remind me of you."

She snort-laughs. "You've been reading too many romance novels, Matthews."

I throw a pillow in her general direction, but since I can't look at her, I'm sure it misses the mark.

She crosses over to the bed and tugs on my arm. "I need coffee. Get your lazy ass out of bed."

I begrudgingly let her pull me off the mattress and into the bathroom. After splashing some water on my face and brushing my teeth, I run my fingers through my hair, not bothering to brush it because I like the way it looks after Jess has had her hands in it. I pull on my own pair of jeans and a sweatshirt and hold the door open for her as we make our way into the hallway.

She stands right next to me in the elevator, our shoulders pressed together. So I take a chance and reach for her hand, tamping down my grin when she laces her fingers through mine. Everything about this morning has brought back all the old feelings—not just the sexy ones, but the soft ones. We feel connected and comfortable. Jess feels like home.

It sounds like a cliché, something I've probably written in one of my books, but nobody ever saw me the way Jess does. I went my whole childhood feeling like an outcast, misunderstood. But with Jess, I never needed to defend myself or explain why I loved the things I do. She just knew, intrinsically, and supported me without question.

When we finally reach the lobby, it's not nearly as full as it has been the past couple of days. Either we're right in the middle of the breakfast and lunch rush, or the weather really did clear up. I know which one I want to be true, but something tells me Jess isn't going to be held captive here at the inn for much longer.

We order our coffees and turn to head to the restaurant to see if we can beg for a late breakfast.

And we almost literally run right into Lauren, SVP's executive director of publicity.

"Nick! Jessica!" Her eyes dart furiously between us, widening as they drop to where our hands are still joined.

I wait for Jess to pull away, but she doesn't, and I tighten my grip in response. "Lauren. Good to see you again. Are you heading home?" I gesture to the suitcase she's pulling along behind her.

She nods. "Yes. Finally. The trains are back up and running, and I've already got a car on the way." She turns to Jess. "Did you want to grab a ride with me to the station? I know you were only supposed to be here for the one night."

Jess sneaks a quick look at me, but I keep my eyes on Lauren, not about to answer for her. "I think I'm going to stay a while longer. Thank you though."

Lauren nods and a genuine smile crosses her face. "Sounds good." She leans in a little closer to Jess, but not close enough that I can't hear. "I really hope whatever is going on here has nothing to do with what we talked about before."

This time I meet Jess's eyes when they dart over to mine. I raise my eyebrows because what the fuck is Lauren talking about?

Jess turns her attention away from me and back to Lauren. "This has absolutely nothing to do with what we discussed. Nick and I, well, we're still figuring it out, to be honest, but whatever is happening here is genuine."

I open my mouth to attempt to get some answers, but Jess squeezes my hand and gives me a *not now* look.

Lauren watches all of this play out, but her emotions are unreadable. "Well, I hope you two are able to figure it out. Please let me know if and when you want to make all of this"—she gestures to the tight grip we have on each other's hands—"public because I will be all over that." Her head cocks to the side. "I wonder if we could get you on *GMA* . . . they love you, Nick, and I think they would eat this story right up. Two romance authors who fell back in love while writing a book together? It's perfection." Her phone lights up in her hand. "My ride is here, but this conversation is not over!" She starts to head for the front door. "Have a great Christmas and let's chat as soon as I'm back in the office!"

Her last words are swallowed up by the automatic doors closing behind her.

For a second we just stand and stare at the place where Lauren stood.

Then I turn to Jess. "Want to tell me what that was all about?"

She sighs and tugs on my hand, pulling me toward the restaurant. "Today is going to be quite the day of reckoning, isn't it? But I need food in my system before we have a whole bunch of serious conversations."

I follow her lead, and after we've been seated and have ordered two huge breakfast platters and another round of coffees, I clasp my hands in front of me on the table. "Do you want to go first?"

"Sure." She takes in a deep breath. "I ran into Lauren in the lobby a couple of days ago and she told me that if you and I were to be in a relationship, it could really help both of our careers."

I reach across the table and take her hand. "Please don't take this the wrong way because I really don't mean to sound like a dick . . ."

"I asked the same thing. I see how it would help me, but how would it benefit you?"

I squeeze her hand, thankful I didn't have to say it out loud. "What did she say?"

"She said that it's time for you to move on to the next phase of your career." She smirks. "Basically she thinks it's time for you to stop being Romancelandia's favorite bachelor. Time for you to settle down and wife up, I guess."

Wifing up doesn't sound so terrible if I'm wifing up Jess.

Jess leans forward in her seat. "Honestly, looking back on it, I might have read too much into our conversation. I know she wasn't actually suggesting we fake date or anything." A smile tugs on her lips, but she tries to hide it with a sip from her coffee. "Maybe I was hearing what I wanted to hear, you know?"

"You wanted an excuse to fake date me?" I can't help but be excited by that declaration. In our world, fake dating is a hop, skip, and a jump away from an HEA.

"I admit nothing."

"Well, I'm glad she didn't actually ask you to fake date me. That would have been extremely inappropriate."

Though if I have anything to say about it, Lauren's greatest PR wishes will all be coming true.

"So you're not mad?"

My brow furrows. "Why would I be mad? Did what happened between us last night have anything to do with your conversation with Lauren?"

"No." Her response is quick and firm.

I shrug and sip my coffee. "Then I have nothing to be mad about."

"Even though I didn't tell you?"

"We weren't together at the time. If it didn't affect your actions, then a conversation with Lauren doesn't matter to me."

"Are we together now?"

The server chooses this very inopportune moment to interrupt us. Of course it isn't until the plate of steaming food is set in front of me that I realize how ravenous I am. I burned a lot of calories last night.

"I really want to answer that question when my stomach is not growling offensively loud."

Jess grins, picking up her fork. "Fine, but don't think you're escaping this conversation. We're just putting it on pause."

"I don't want to escape this conversation, Jess." I want to tell her everything. I need to tell her everything. All I can do is hope she'll give me another chance after she knows the whole story.

NICK

I wake up Christmas morning with a stomach full of butterflies. Today is going to be one of the most important days of my life, and while the lead-up has held nothing but excitement, I'd be lying if I said there wasn't an equal amount of anxiety swirling around in my gut.

There's a ring nestled in a little black velvet box hidden in my underwear drawer. I knew the moment I saw it in the store window that it would be perfect for her. That it was *the* ring.

And even though my contract hasn't been officially signed yet, and I haven't received my advance, I know the money is coming, so I let myself splurge.

When I talked to Jess's parents a few weeks ago—not so much to ask permission because Jess is a grown woman who can decide for herself, but because I wanted to share the news with the people closest to her—they both cried over FaceTime, telling me they couldn't wait for me to officially be their son.

I'd been able to choke back the tears until we hung up, but I hope they know how much it meant to me, to have their support. Support that has been unwavering and unconditional, unlike the recent support I've suddenly been blessed with from my own family.

A couple of weeks ago, I called to tell them that not only are my books going to be published, but I received an offer for a life-changing amount of money. They never understood my writing or my love of romance novels, but they definitely understand the words "six figures." I don't even think it's the money, necessarily, more that this is a tangible sign of success. When I made the decision to "abandon" the family business and pursue my own dreams, no one was really surprised. Despite the grooming my brothers and I went through as kids, it was always clear I never quite fit in at Matthews and Sons Construction. Moving to New York, according to my parents, was risky and a financially dumb decision. Why would I chance an unpredictable career like writing when I had a sure thing being handed to me?

Normally, conversations with my family end with one or both of my parents pleading for me to come home, to come work a "real" job. This latest conversation ended with my dad telling me he was proud of me for I think the first time ever. I want to pretend like I didn't need to hear those words. But I did.

The one person who has been happiest for me over these past couple of whirlwind weeks is Jess. I'm sure it can't have always been easy to see me getting everything we've both been working so hard for, but she has never once let her support falter or her smile waver. She has been there with me through every single second, even when my indecision about which deal to accept was likely driving her to the brink of insanity.

Luckily, in maybe the most fortuitous gift of good timing ever, Jess also got an offer. Only one, and more modest than mine, but with SVP, an incredible romance publisher whom I also ended up deciding to sign with.

A Christmas engagement should be the cherry on top of this life-goals sundae we've been digging into over the past few weeks.

So why is my stomach a sinking pit of dread?

I've spent the past two weeks mulling over a conversation I had with Marcus, the only person aside from Jess who can really understand what this opportunity means to me. We've been friends for so long, he's seen me through every phase of my writing career.

When he made an offhand comment about how many more books I might sell if I were single—a sort of real-life book boyfriend—I didn't take him too seriously. Marcus is in marketing, and I know by now he's always looking for the next gimmick, the next way to go viral and sell big. He's been able to do it for his clients more than once in the past, but it's not like anything is ever guaranteed, so it was easy to shrug off his implications.

But when he mentioned how my success might overshadow Jess, I couldn't dismiss that so easily. The publishing industry isn't exactly transparent, but it doesn't take a genius to figure out that, with the difference in the size of our advances, my book will be getting the lion's share of SVP's focus. And then there's the real tough question—what if our relationship makes people question just how Jess got her deal—like SVP is doing me some kind of favor by publishing my girlfriend's books alongside mine.

It's been ruminating in my mind ever since that night at our favorite dive bar. I haven't spoken about it with anyone, haven't wanted to even bring it up again with Marcus, afraid he might provide me with even more compelling reasons why the greatest achievement of my life so far might be putting a damper on hers.

The more I consider all angles, the more I think Marcus might be right. Being tied to me could end up hurting Jess's career, and I can't think of anything in the world I want less.

There's also a small part of me, a part I hate to even acknowledge, but it's there, that knows Marcus is right about the other thing too. I can see how being single—being "attainable"—could help me sell more books.

If you had asked me a month ago if I would even think about trading my relationship with Jess to sell more books, I would have laughed at the mere suggestion.

Jess is everything to me.

Or she was, until that offer landed in my inbox. Until all of my dreams were suddenly within reach. Until my dad told me he was proud. Shame heats my cheeks at the very thought.

I know I should just tell her my concerns. I should let her know what Marcus said, let her be the one to decide if she would rather have a career where she can stand on her own merits, unencumbered by me.

I shake that thought out of my head. I know Jess. Her whole life revolves around love. She isn't the type to pick a career over true love, or at least that's what I keep telling myself. I don't know if it makes me feel better or worse at this point.

I turn on my side, watching as Jess's chest rises and falls. A tiny smile tugs on the corner of her lips, and I hope that means she's having a good dream. The kind of dream where she gets everything she wants in life.

I slip out of bed, careful not to disturb her, tiptoeing past the living room where Alyssa and Kennedy sleep on an air mattress. In the kitchen of our one-bedroom apartment, I prep her coffee. In addition to splurging on a ring, I also bought us an espresso machine so Jess can make her disgustingly sweet coffee drinks from the comfort of our home. I even bought peppermint and chocolate syrups, even though the smell of peppermint makes me want to gag.

Jess's love of Christmas isn't going anywhere; it's one of the reasons I picked today to propose.

I pour myself a mug of black coffee. Actually, that's a lie, I throw a splash of whiskey in there because something tells me I'm going to need a little liquid courage.

Once Jess's overly sweet drink is prepared, I take both mugs into the bedroom, setting hers on the night table before leaning down to place a soft kiss on her forehead.

She blinks up at me sleepily, that soft smile growing as she drinks me in. "Good morning."

"Good morning." I gesture to the coffee waiting for her before climbing back into bed next to her.

"Mmm. Peppermint mocha in bed on Christmas morning. Is it too soon to declare this the best Christmas ever?" She sits up, wrapping her hands around the mug and drinking deeply.

I laugh, hoping it doesn't sound as hollow to her as it does to me. "Alyssa and Kennedy are still asleep."

"Good. The three of us were up way too late last night." She sets her mug on the nightstand so she can pull the covers up to her chin. "We had lots to catch up on."

"Are they excited for your deal?"

A shadow darkens the golden brown of her eyes. "Of course."

There's a lot more there that she's not saying, but I figure she doesn't want to spill her friends' secrets, so I don't push for more details.

We cuddle in bed until we hear the girls stirring in the living room. Kennedy makes us breakfast, and after a walk around the neighborhood, we spend the afternoon watching Christmas movies and drinking hot chocolate. The whole thing would be idyllic if it weren't for the life-changing question I'm planning on asking later and the sudden bout of indecision I've been plagued with.

Jess decided a couple of days ago that she wanted to make a full Christmas dinner, and so early in the afternoon, she and Alyssa head into the kitchen. Kennedy is on deadline and takes the time to get some words in.

I use this brief respite to hide out in the bedroom and reread the latest string of emails from my agent.

I was lucky to have my pick of agents when I was querying, and Stacy is the best. She's ruthless and cutthroat, and always gives me a straight answer. A couple of days ago, I explained the whole situation, how I'm worried my success is going to get in the way of Jess's chance, how I don't want to be the one to take anything away from her. How much I would hate it if anyone were to suggest the only reason she got published was because of her connections to me.

And yeah, I threw in the part about me and my marketability too, just at the end, so she knows that's not my main concern.

Her reply didn't mince words, much as I expected. She confirmed Marcus's observation, that being single could help me sell a ton more books, maybe even make me a household name. She didn't seem as concerned with the whole *me overshadowing Jess* bit, probably because Jess isn't her client so it doesn't affect her much.

My eyes keep drifting back to the phrase "household name." It's honestly not something I ever really thought to want. How many writers end up being household names?

But Stacy thinks the potential is there for me, that I could be one of those select few.

My phone buzzes with a text, and I swipe out of my email.

MOM: Merry Christmas, sweetheart! Hope you're having a great day and taking some time to enjoy the spoils of your success!

The message brings a smile to my face, even though I know it probably shouldn't. Where was this support three years ago when I really needed it? I'm pretty sure I didn't even get a text last Christmas.

DAD: Merry Christmas, son. Proud of you.

And yeah, Mom likely told him to send the message, but he sent it.

I toss my phone aside and cross the room to the dresser. The ring has been hidden in my underwear drawer for weeks, and when I take it out, the roiling in my stomach feels a lot more like dread than it does excitement.

I shove it back into the deepest corner of the drawer. Marrying Jess is the right thing. It has to be.

After attempting to read for a bit, even though my brain can't focus on any of the words, I head toward the kitchen to see if I can offer assistance. Our kitchen isn't big enough for more than two people, but I know I should at least offer to help.

I hold back in the hallway when I hear my name.

"Nick isn't the kind of guy who's going to let success go to his head." Alyssa's defense of my character is reassuring, even though I don't know where the need for it came from.

"I know that." Jess.

Has she been thinking the same kind of things I have been?

"I'm so happy for him, guys, truly," she continues. "I know how hard he has worked for this moment, and he's so talented, and so deserving."

"But?" Kennedy pushes her to finish the thought, and I'm grateful she does, knowing I need to hear it.

"But it's been really hard these past couple of weeks. Seeing every major publisher fight over his book. Seeing the kinds of things they're promising him, the amount of money they're willing to throw at him. They designed a whole marketing plan already, even before he signed his contract, basically promised him he'll be a bestseller. And he deserves it all, truly."

"We know that as well as you do. And having these kinds of thoughts doesn't make you a bad or unsupportive girlfriend," Alyssa says.

Some part of me has known how hard this must be for Jess, but she's done nothing but smile and support me, and I hate myself for not bringing it up myself, for letting her stew in her feelings without me there to support her in turn.

"I don't know if I can do it," Jess says quietly. "I don't know if I can go the whole rest of my career playing second fiddle. And I hate myself for that, for even entertaining the thought. I love him so much, but I don't know if I can do it. I don't know if I can be with him."

Her voice breaks, and so does my heart.

It's the final push I need. I know she won't let herself end our relationship because of this—she's too good of a person. But I can be the one to do it for her.

Even if it kills me.

Chapter Twenty-One

JESS

I eat slowly, despite being so hungry it feels like my stomach is devouring itself. I want to enjoy these last few moments with Nick, where everything is calm and peaceful and the hurt feelings are far in the past.

I have a feeling once he explains why he chose to break up with me that those hurt feelings will be back in full force. Because what could he possibly tell me, what could possibly justify cutting me off and breaking my heart? Destroying everything we had together, right as our dreams were coming true?

We make small talk as we eat, jibe at each other and crack jokes, the sting softened by a wide smile and the squeeze of a hand.

Nick charges the meal to his room and then pushes back his chair. "Should we head upstairs?"

I shake my head, pushing back my own chair and leading him out into the lobby. "Don't take this the wrong way, but I don't think it's a good idea for us to be in close proximity to a bed when we are meant to be talking about the serious things."

He wraps his arm around my waist, tugging me closer and planting a kiss on the top of my head. "How could I take that in any other way but the best way? It means you can't resist me."

I roll my eyes, but I don't pull away. "I think we both know you are the one who can't resist me."

"Yes, but I would never dare say otherwise. You know I've never been able to deny you anything, Jess."

Except for a satisfying explanation of what broke us up.

I take him over to the quiet corner of the lobby I discovered earlier in the week, though the entire lobby is much quieter now that the hotel's occupants have been able to head home. With how badly I wanted to get out of here, it's hard to believe I voluntarily turned down a ride to the train station.

That's the power of Nick Matthews, I suppose.

We settle into our armchairs, the two of us still close enough that I can feel the warmth radiating from him, but with enough space that I should be able to think clearly.

Nick leans forward in his chair, his elbows resting on his knees. "I'm not sure where to start."

"How about we start with the why? Did your feelings for me change? Were you concerned about me dragging down your career somehow? Did you feel like you'd outgrown me, that I was no longer enough for you?" The questions come spilling out of me, and I didn't realize how much I was still holding in. Before this week, I would have told you I was well and truly over Nick, that our breakup was an unfortunate incident firmly in my past. But the rush of emotion rising in my chest and the wetness springing up in my eyes would tell the truth.

"No, Jess. God no. None of that." He scrubs his hands over the thighs of his jeans and looks at me, his hazel eyes full of a hundred emotions. I want to separate them all out and dissect each one.

"Then why?" I whisper, swallowing the tears before they have the chance to trail down my cheeks.

"I need you to know, first and foremost, that my feelings for you were real and true. I saw a future for us." His voice drops and he turns his gaze away from me. "I went ring shopping and I talked to your parents."

I suck in a breath. All of that is news to me. "They never told me." I know them well enough to know it's not a betrayal; they just didn't want me to suffer any more than I already was.

He nods. "I'm not surprised. I asked them to keep it a secret and then, well, then everything changed."

I'm sick of asking for further clarification so I just sit in silence until he works up the nerve to speak again.

"There's no way to put this that doesn't make me sound like the asshole that I was. The asshole I would like to think I no longer am."

"I'll be the judge of that."

A small smile tugs on his lips. "Fair enough." He sits back in his chair. "At the time, I pretty much talked myself into breaking up with you for your own good."

My mouth drops open, but I don't bother speaking, letting him continue to dig this hole all on his own.

"I had a conversation with Marcus, about how our relationship might come off to readers. I don't think he ever meant me to take it so seriously, but it really got in my head. This idea that if we stayed together, people might think I was the reason you got your book deal." He runs a hand through his hair. "The last thing I wanted at that point in time was for anything having to do with my deal to overshadow yours, or to take opportunities away from you. I asked Stacy for her perspective, her professional insight, and she confirmed everything Marcus told me."

I purse my lips, my head shaking back and forth.

"But the worst part, Jess, the part that makes me feel like you would be justified to never forgive me, is the other part of what Marcus told me. That I would be much more marketable, would sell more books, if I were single."

"So you broke up with me because your best friend—who, by the way, does not work in publishing, and as far as I know has never read a romance novel—came up with a marketing idea?" I don't sound as angry as I want to, maybe because a huge part of me can't believe what I'm hearing. He gave up the supposed love of his life so he could sell more books?

He grimaces. "That was the start of it."

I cock my head to the side, as if that can help me see inside his brain. "And what was the rest of it?"

He lets out a long sigh. "Like I said, Stacy reinforced what Marcus said, about both of us. How it would be better for both of our careers if we weren't involved with one another. I didn't see it at the time, but maybe her motivation had more to do with me selling more books rather than protecting you."

I know him well enough to know he's still holding something back. "And?"

His eyes meet mine and they are layered with sadness. "And I heard you talking to Alyssa and Kennedy, in the kitchen on our last Christmas together."

It takes a minute for the conversation to come back to me, but I don't have to rehash it in my mind because Nick seems to remember the whole thing word for word.

"You were talking about how hard it was for you to be by my side at that moment in our careers. You said you didn't think you could do it." He leans forward, resting his elbows on his knees, his head drooping, his eyes avoiding mine. "I would do a hundred things differently if I could go back and change the past, but not if it meant you ended up resenting me. You were always the one person who saw me, who got me, and I couldn't bear to lose that. Letting you go killed me, Jess, but somehow, I think that would have been worse."

My cheeks are wet. "So it was my fault?"

"No. Absolutely not." Nick reaches for one of my hands, and I let him take it. "I should have talked with you first. I should have told you how I was feeling, and listened, really listened to what you were feeling too." He chuckles, but there's no humor in it. "I guess you were right about couples sucking at communication."

"It's not an easy thing to do, for anyone." That truth doesn't make me feel any better.

"Even though I won't deny I had some selfish motivations, I really did think about you and your career, and what would be best." His thumb strokes my knuckles and it's almost hypnotizing how his touch can soothe me.

"But you should have let me be the one to make that decision." I release his hand. "And at this point we both know, being single, never being connected to one another publicly, well, it's worked out great for you. I can't sit here and say it's done much for me."

Would this be easier to digest if my career had soared without Nick? Something tells me it wouldn't.

"I know."

At least he doesn't try to placate me with false platitudes.

"This week, Jess, being able to spend time with you and reconnect with you, it's reminded me of everything we had. It's reminded me of how much I loved you then, and I think it's shown me, more than anything else, how much I love you still."

I look up just in time to catch him swiping at his own cheeks. "This is all a lot to process."

"I know."

"And now, no matter what happens with us, no matter where we decide to go with our relationship, we've written a book together." My stomach spins, just as fast as my brain is tumbling. Everything that has happened over the past few days is swirling around in my head and my heart, and I don't know how to make sense of any of it.

There's anger and frustration about our past, and I'm unsure if it's outweighed by the way we've fit so easily back together. Yes, I now know the truth, and know it's a truth I can find a way to move past, but who's to say the same thing might not happen again in the future? How do I know Nick has changed?

"If you want the book, you can have it, Jess. If this is where it ends, if you don't want to see me again after this, you can have the book. I'll tell everyone we tried to write together and it didn't work, and you can keep the entire thing."

I shake my head. "I'm not putting my name on your work, Nick. And besides, we still have to come up with an ending."

"Is it too hard to see a way for our characters to come back together? Can they have a real second chance?" We both know he isn't talking about our characters.

"I don't know."

"So where do we go from here?" His hand moves, like he wants to reach for me again but is holding himself back.

"I think I need to go home."

The hurt in his eyes hurts me too, and I realize how far I've fallen over the past couple of days. But I can't think like this, trapped here in this holiday hotel with him, surrounded by nothing but warm fuzzies. I need space, a chance to get my head together without him influencing me.

"Okay. If that's what you need."

I nod and rise from my chair. "I'm going to go upstairs and pack."

"I'll wait for you here."

I head toward the elevators, looking back once. Nick has fully sunk into the armchair, his head in his hands like it's too heavy to hold up. He looks about as broken as I feel.

I don't have much stuff and so it only takes me a few minutes to throw everything into my bag. I change out of Nick's sweatshirt, and yeah, I might hold the soft fabric to my nose, breathing in the pine and juniper scent of him before folding it up and leaving it on the bed. Pulling on my slightly smelly sweater, I do one more check to make sure I haven't forgotten anything.

Nick has moved from the quiet corner when I make my way back down to the lobby, waiting for me in front of the massive Christmas tree.

He always was the best part of Christmas.

I ask the front desk to call me a taxi and leave my bag with them while I make my way over to the man I thought might be mine once again. I don't resist when he pulls me into his arms. I bury myself in his warmth, in his scent, in the strength of his hands on my back.

"I really hope this isn't goodbye," he murmurs into my neck. "Even if we're just friends, I want you in my life, Jess."

"I don't know if I can be just friends with you, Nick." I wrap my arms around his neck, rising on my toes to bring me closer. "I don't know if this is goodbye, I just know I need some time to think."

"Take all the time you need. I'm here whenever you're ready."

I tilt my head up, and he brings his lips down to mine. The kiss is soft and sweet, gentle and knowing. It's the comfort of a cozy blanket and the heat of a fire stoking deep in my belly.

At a honk from outside, I pull myself away reluctantly. Leaving him is the right thing to do, but it certainly doesn't feel like it in this moment. I wave to the cab to let them know I'm on my way. "I should go."

He brushes a thumb along my cheek. "Get home safely." He leans down, his mouth hovering a fraction of an inch from mine.

He waits for me to close the space, and I do, placing one final kiss, just a breath of a touch, on his lips.

"Have a good Christmas, Jess."

"Yeah, you too." I spin on my heel and walk away, forcing myself not to look back.

My brain is a mess, but my heart is cracking in two. This time I'm the one walking away, but it doesn't feel any better.

Chapter Twenty-Two

NICK

Watching her walk away from me—again—is the hardest thing I've ever had to do. I feel like I'm watching a piece of myself breaking away, pulling away from me, and leaving me with a Jess-shaped hole in my chest.

I sink into the closest armchair in the lobby, not wanting to head back to my room in case she changes her mind and comes back. I know she's not going to, but that doesn't stop me from checking the front door every thirty seconds, just to be sure.

I don't know how long I've been sitting there when a hand lands on my shoulder. "You're still here."

I finally pull my eyes away from the front door and turn to look at my editor, Gina. "Still here."

Her brow furrows. "Everything okay? You look like someone just told you Santa's not real."

"What do you mean Santa's not real?" I inject false humor into my voice, not really wanting to get into this whole situation with someone who is, in some ways, my boss.

"Okay, that might convince someone who hasn't spent hours and hours with you working out character development." She sits in the chair across from mine. "What's going on?"

"I think I just had my heart broken." I know I shouldn't confide this in her, should keep our relationship professional, but she's here and I know she cares about my mental well-being—at least as much as it pertains to me being a functioning writer.

"Ah. The real-life second-chance romance didn't play out the way it would in a book, huh?"

"Maybe it played out exactly like it would in one of my books. And that's the problem."

Gina settles back in her chair and levels me with a look. "You know, I hate editing the endings of your books."

Not much could snap me out of this funk, but hearing my editor—someone I consider my partner in this whole writing game—tell me she hates a major part of my books does the trick. "You hate the endings?"

She nods, lacing her fingers together and resting them in her lap.

"Then why do you let me write them?"

"It's not my place to tell you what to write. I'm here to make your books better, Nick. Make your plots stronger and your characters deeper. But I'm not here to change something that's so fundamentally who you are as a writer."

"The funny thing is, it's not who I was as a writer. At least it wasn't in the beginning." I think back to the days when all my stories ended happily. I loved finding the thing that broke my characters apart, but I loved putting them back together even more.

"What about this new book? The holiday second-chance romance. Did you and Jess end up collaborating?"

"We did. I don't know where the project is going to go, though. I think that's kind of up to her." I tap my fingers on my knee. "We still have to figure out how it ends."

"I think you know how it ends." She straightens the hem of her pencil skirt, which she's wearing even though we're technically trapped on a work vacation. "Would it help if I told you I may have mentioned the idea to the higher-ups while I was forced to dine with them against my will, and they loved it?"

"How much did they love it?" It doesn't matter for me so much, but I know what this could do for Jess.

"Enough to get your girl off the midlist." She stands, adjusting her shirt, though not a stitch is out of place. "I'll be in touch with more after the holidays. Now might be time to start planning your grand gesture."

"What do you mean?"

She rolls her eyes. "You know, that thing that's missing from most of your books, when the person who messed up—usually the hero, if we're being honest—does something big and impressive to prove how much they love the other person? It's the thing that leads to all those happily ever afters."

"And you think I need one? To get Jess back?"

"Certainly couldn't hurt." She pats my cheek. "You also might want to think about shaving."

"Haha." I capture her hand with mine and squeeze

tightly. "Thank you, Gina. I really appreciate you and I hope you have a good holiday."

"Thanks to your book sales and my resulting holiday bonus, I usually do." She throws a wink over her shoulder as she heads out the front door. "Do what you need to do to write a good story for yourself, Nick."

Chapter Twenty-Three

JESS

s there anything more depressing than coming home to an empty house two days before Christmas feeling absolutely destroyed, mentally and emotionally?

That's a rhetorical question.

I let myself into my apartment after an hour-and-a-half train ride and a subway transfer and a ten-minute walk through the brisk cold, my overnight bag slung over my arm, a literal weight on my shoulder to mimic the figurative one in my heart. The snow is no longer pouring down from the heavens, but it still litters the sidewalks, and the gray sky still hangs heavy and foreboding. But the weather doesn't matter much at this point. I'm back at home with nowhere to go and no one to see.

Actually, that's not entirely true. I'm still scheduled for a shift at the coffee shop tomorrow, a real jolt back to reality. As much as so much of this past week sucked, it was a glimpse at life as a full-time writer, a glimpse I sort of hate to give up. But I text Morgan to let her know I'm back in town and that I'll be in tomorrow, before I can let myself dwell on it too much. I need the money, and tips should be good on Christmas Eve.

After a long hot shower, I put on my coziest sweats and climb into bed. It's not even close to bedtime yet, but I don't really care at this point. I need comfort and reality TV escapism, and to not think about Nick Matthews for a few minutes.

Ha.

Like that's going to happen.

Once I get a vintage episode of *Real Housewives* going, I take out my phone and open my very much neglected text chain with Alyssa and Kennedy.

ME: I made it back home!

Maybe the exclamation point will fool them into thinking I'm totally fine.

ALYSSA: Yay!!! How was the rest of the time at the inn?

We both know what she's asking, but I love her for not coming right out and saying it.

ME: It was fine.

Ten seconds later, my phone rings with a request for a FaceTime. I sigh, pausing the show so I can answer the call. When it connects, both of my best friends are there on the screen, wearing almost identical looks, though Alyssa's holds a tinge more sympathy while Kennedy's firmly says *I told you so.*

"Spill," Kennedy directs.

There is no denying her. "We slept together."

They take in a collective breath.

"He told me he's still in love with me, has always been in love with me, really."

Alyssa swoons. "Ohmygod, that is the most romantic thing I've ever heard of in real life! You two got trapped together in a cozy Christmas inn, you only had one bed, and your second-chance romance ended with him telling you he's always loved you!"

Kennedy clears her throat. "In case you missed it, Lys, she's sitting in her bed in sweats by herself. Something tells me that's not exactly how it ended."

Alyssa's eyes widen, but she doesn't say anything.

"Yeah, unfortunately this didn't exactly play out like it would in one of our books." I reach for the glass of wine I wisely brought into bed with me and take a long swig. "I think I might be living a real-life Nick Matthews ending."

"What happened?" Kennedy asks quietly.

"If I'm being honest, there was a moment there, maybe more than a moment, when I thought we were going to end up back together." I take another drink. "But then he told me the reason he broke up with me five years ago."

"The sex was so good you thought you might get back together?" Kennedy interjects, bringing some much-needed lightness to the conversation.

"God yes. It was incredible." I have to clench my thighs together just thinking about it.

"Good sex is great, and necessary, but I want to know more about what he told you," Alyssa says. "What exactly did he say that was so terrible?"

I blow out a short breath. "It was a many-pronged explanation, but the real crux of it is that his friend Marcus, who works in marketing, told him he would probably sell a lot more books if he was single and could play up the whole *real-life book boyfriend* angle."

Kennedy's lips purse so tightly I'm afraid she'll never be able to separate them, but then she does. "What the fuck?"

"He actually said that to you?" Alyssa's voice is soft and tinged with worry.

"He also said he thought there was a chance that if I was publicly connected to him, it would overshadow my own success. Like people might think I only got published because I'm dating him."

Kennedy's brow scrunches. "Do you think he really thought that or is that just an excuse to make him not look so completely terrible?"

I shrug, but I know in my heart Nick wasn't lying. "I don't doubt that that's how he felt in the moment."

"I don't think he would lie about the breakup, not if at the same time he's telling you that he always loved you." Alyssa and Nick hung out several times while we were dating, and she always did adore him. I think she was just as devastated when he dumped me as I was.

"There's one other thing." I finish my glass of wine for liquid courage. "He overheard us in the kitchen, that Christmas right before we signed our contracts, when we'd both already gotten our deals."

Kennedy's look of confusion makes it clear she doesn't remember, but Alyssa's sympathetic smile shows she does.

"You said you didn't know if you could do it," she says quietly.

I nod. "Yup. Maybe if he hadn't overheard me saying that, he never would have broken up with me in the first place. Maybe the whole thing is all my fault."

"He should have talked to you about it first." Kennedy defends my honor, like I knew she would.

"He was probably feeling hurt and didn't know how to broach the subject with her." Alyssa fights for love, like I knew she would.

"Still, taking everything into account, he should have been mature enough to have an honest conversation. If he really thought he might be hurting Jess's career, he should have explained that to her and let her decide what she wanted to do. He didn't have the right to make that choice for her." Kennedy walks into her own kitchen and pours herself a glass of wine. Good to know my problems are so bad my friends need to drink to help me handle them.

"No way," Alyssa argues. "How could he put her in that position, forcing her to choose between him and the success she'd always wanted? It would have been an impossible choice, and if Jess had to make it, it would have caused her a lot of pain."

"But it was still her choice. She had the right to make it, not him."

Alyssa shakes her head. "Nope. He did the right thing by bowing out, even if there were other, more selfish motivations at play too."

"He broke her heart!"

"Hi, friends. I am still, in fact, sitting right here while you argue over the merits of my career and relationship status."

Both of them look appropriately shamed.

I sigh. "Look. Assuming Nick really was conflicted about the whole career thing, I don't really know what the best choice would have been. Honestly, I think if he had presented me with the situation, I probably would have chosen him, even if I did think it would hurt my book sales." And then, chances are, I would have had the same disappointing career I do now, but I would also have had the man I love by my side for the past five years.

Kennedy wrinkles her nose. Alyssa swoons.

"And then I would have probably grown to resent him, standing by his side watching him get all the things I'm still waiting for." I know as I speak the words, that they are undoubtedly true. If I was already struggling at the outset, how would I have felt watching Nick achieve everything he's achieved over the past few years while I continued to struggle? I'd like to think I would have been happy for him, and I'm sure a large part of me would have—hell, even broken up, I still have looked at his career accomplishments with pride. But there would have been envy too, and I don't know that that envy wouldn't have eaten away at us.

Maybe Nick really did do us a favor.

A silence falls between the three of us.

"So what do I do now?" I ask after a quiet minute.

"I don't think we can answer that for you," Kennedy says. "Has enough really changed since then? What would be different this time around?"

"I think you just need to take care of yourself. It's almost Christmas. Maybe you should take tonight to wallow, but spend tomorrow doing some of your favorite holiday things."

I nod at Alyssa's suggestion, knowing I will be spending a good chunk of the day tomorrow serving people their holiday drinks while they go about their merry lives, not mired in thoughts of Christmases past.

"Whatever you decide to do, you know we're here." Kennedy raises her glass to me, a virtual toast.

"I know. Thank you, guys, really. You're the best."

"We know."

I wave and blow them both kisses before exiting from the call and turning back to the *Real Housewives*. Burrowing deeper into bed, I pull the covers all the way up to my chin. I don't know what to make of the conversation with my friends, other than no one can really tell me what to do in this situation. I know Kennedy's right about one thing— I need to really think about what's changed, not just for Nick, but for me too. If we give this thing a real shot, am I in a good enough place now where I can handle the differences in our careers?

In the meantime, because I have gifted myself this period of wallowing, I allow myself to really sink into it. My bed is very cold and could certainly benefit from a very hot and hunky writer warming the sheets next to me. Has my bed always been this big? It feels a lot emptier all of a sudden.

Ugh. The last thing I need to be doing right now is thinking about Nick Matthews in my bed. If we hadn't ended up in a room with only one bed, none of this would have happened. This shit is not supposed to happen in real life.

I'm about to go pour myself some more wine—and by that I mean grab the bottle and bring it back with me— when my phone dings with a text.

I expect it to be Alyssa, gracing me with some cheerful words of wisdom, but it's not one of my friends' names that I see on the screen.

NICK: Did you make it home safely?

I really wish the sight of his name didn't send a whirl of snowflakes fluttering through my chest.

ME: Yup. Home and in bed with a glass of wine and the Real Housewives.

And maybe I should be laying off the wine because he definitely didn't need to know any of that.

NICK: Your favorite place to be. I'm glad you made it back in time for Christmas. I'm sure you've got big plans for your favorite holiday.

ME: I don't have plans for Christmas Day, actually. Alyssa was supposed to come up before the storm canceled her flight, and my parents are out of town.

ME: But none of that matters to you because we are supposed to be not talking right now.

I type and send the message, but I don't really feel any truth in the words. If anything, I find myself wanting to talk to him.

NICK: Shit. I'm sorry. You told me you need space and I fully plan to give it to you.

NICK: I just miss you already.

NICK: And I'm sorry, again. For everything.

NICK: Have a merry Christmas, Jess.

ME: Yeah. You too.

My fingers dig into the sides of my phone, and it's a good thing it's made of strong stuff because my grip is so tight I'm surprised the whole thing doesn't snap in half.

He misses me.

It's easy to believe that part of it, because even though I don't really want to admit it to myself, I miss him too. Having Nick back in my life, just for a few short days, was enough to remind me how good we were together. And even if I can't end up forgiving him, or if it does turn out neither of us has grown enough to be able to come back together in a healthy relationship, it doesn't change the fact that I really loved him.

That I might love him still.

I jump up from my bed, thankful that I am the kind of person who never immediately unpacks after returning from a trip because it means my laptop is still in my bag at the foot of my bed. I grab my computer and bring it with me back under the covers.

Nick and I still haven't figured out how we want to end our story, but right now, I'm in the perfect mental state to write a devastating third-act breakup.

Chapter Twenty-Four

NICK

The moment I'm back in the quiet of my hotel room after saying goodbye to Gina, I take out my phone, but I'm not sure who I want to call. Marcus would be the obvious choice, but we're not the kind of friends who talk about emotions, not real ones. And part of this is his fault.

I could call Hilary, but technically she is on vacation, and while I'm sure she would listen, and willingly so, I can't help but shake the feeling that she would only pick up the phone because I'm her boss.

I sink onto the side of the hotel bed, my phone still in my hand. Before I give myself the chance to fully consider what I'm doing, I pull up my mom's cell number and dial.

"Nicky!" She answers right away, the brightness in her voice genuine. "I wasn't expecting to hear from you until Christmas."

"I hope it's okay that I called."

"Of course it's okay. You can call anytime. You know that."

I do know that. Even if things haven't always been great

between us, I've never doubted that my family would be there if I really needed them. I just haven't ever really taken them up on that offer of support. Partly because of lingering resentment from my childhood, but also partly because I've never wanted to give them the chance to be there for me.

"Is everything okay?" my mom asks after a minute of silence.

I let out a long sigh. "I'm not sure, Mom. Something happened this week, and I was hoping I could maybe get your advice."

"I don't know if I have any good advice, but if nothing else, I'm willing to listen."

She's willing to listen, and so I talk. I tell her everything, about the breakup from five years ago, the way I've never been able to fully move on, what it felt like to see Jess again, the creative spark of writing with her, and most importantly, how it felt watching her walk away.

My mom listens, giving me her full attention and plenty of sympathetic sounds.

"And she asked for space, and I want to make sure I respect that, but I also want her to know how much she means to me, and that I'm willing to do whatever she needs to make it work between us," I finally finish.

"Is there a way you can give her space and do this grand gesture thing you were talking about?"

"I don't know. I don't even have a single idea for a grand gesture as it is."

She laughs. "You're the romance writer. I'm sure you can think of something."

"What if she can't forgive me? I basically chose career

over love—it's unforgiveable." I voice my fears aloud for the first time. I know what I did was wrong. I know I would change things if I could. But that doesn't mean Jess is obligated to forgive me. Even if she can move past it, maybe she won't want to.

"I think there are a lot of reasons you put your career first in that situation, Nicky, and I think a lot of that is probably my fault." She takes in a long breath, and I can hear the emotion clouding her voice. "I don't think I did a very good job letting you know that I love and accept you no matter what, and that you've always made me so proud. I don't care how many books you've sold, I don't care if you never sell another single copy in the future. Your dad and I couldn't be prouder of you. You're my son, and I love you."

I have to blink away my own tears, because even though I've never truly doubted the sentiment, it still does something to me, to hear it out loud. "Thank you for saying that."

"I'm sorry I didn't say it sooner. I know I only met Jess once, but I could tell from the moment I met her that she was the one for you, and I think if you have a chance, you should make sure you don't waste it."

"Thanks, Mom."

"Let me know how it goes."

"I will." I only hesitate for a second. "I love you."

"I love you too, my sweet boy."

It takes me several minutes after hanging up the phone before I'm ready to even think about the next steps. For so long, I thought my family pushed me away, couldn't accept me for who I was. But maybe in reality, I've pushed them to the side because it felt like the easiest thing to do. Maybe I needed to let them be there for me, in whatever capacity.

I know one conversation isn't going to fix a lifetime of experiences, but it did show me one thing: People can change.

I open my laptop, pulling up the Google doc. I scroll to the end, sucking in a sharp breath when I see Jess has added a whole chapter since leaving the hotel.

Leaning back on the pillows of the bed, with sheets that still smell like her winter jasmine perfume, I read what she's written.

The breakup scene.

It's nothing short of devastating, the kind of scene you read with a physical ache in your chest. The characters' emotions are so real, it's like I'm experiencing the split right along with them.

At the end of the chapter, Jess has typed two final words: *The End.*

I guess she wants to go along with a Nick Matthews ending.

But as I read the chapter again, I know that this isn't right. This isn't how the story should end, for our characters or for us.

It comes to me in a flash. What I need to do. The grand gesture, so to speak.

I reach for my phone again, this time dialing Hilary's number without hesitation. "I know it's two days before Christmas, but I really need your help and I promise I will give you the biggest bonus you've ever gotten if you can help me pull this off and make this the most magical Christmas ever."

Hilary is quiet for a second. "Did you just say you want to make this the most magical Christmas ever?"

I laugh. "Yes."

"Who are you and what have you done with Nick Matthews?"

"I know this sounds ridiculous, but I really need your help."

"Oh honey, you had my help at 'biggest bonus you've ever gotten.' What do you need me to do?"

I explain the plan and what exactly I'll need from her to make it all, well, go to plan. Before we even hang up the phone, I can hear her keyboard clacking as she furiously googles or emails or works whatever assistant magic she wields so easily.

And so I sit down to do my part. I open a blank document and I write. I write and I write and I write, barely stopping to pee and shove some room service dinner in my face.

I write well into the night, and then into the morning hours. I write so many words I lose count. I write for so long, the words on the screen start to blend together into fuzzy little dots. I save our book, our story, for last, and when I finish it, I know this is the way it was always supposed to end.

That's when I finally save the document and send it off to the contact Hilary found for me. It's going to cost me a fortune to get it done on time, and I'll have to take the first morning train back to the city to make the pick-up window, but I know it will be worth it. It's the early morning of Christmas Eve and I can't keep my eyes open for one second longer. I fall into the bed, noticing how much colder it is without Jess there huddled up on the other side, hogging all the covers but giving off so much warmth it doesn't really matter.

I miss her.

But if everything goes as it should, as it does in the books and the movies that she—that we—love so much, then she'll be back in my arms tomorrow.

For the first time in my life, I can't wait for Christmas.

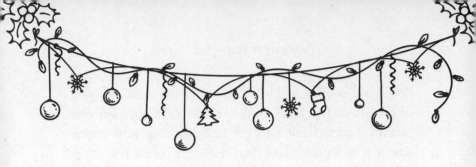

Chapter Twenty-Five

JESS

When I wake up on Christmas Eve, I'm actually grateful I've been scheduled for the early shift. I need a distraction, and nothing is a better distraction than a line full of customers who need a caffeine boost. Morgan, to no one's surprise, is extremely cool about my missing the past few days of work. She accepts my apology by tossing me an apron and shooing me behind the counter, where I spend the rest of the morning making more peppermint mochas than even I can stomach.

I offer to stay late, cover the afternoon shift as well, but Morgan practically pushes me out the front door with a wish for a merry Christmas.

And with that, I'm left to my own devices for the rest of the holiday. I decide to take my friends' advice because, honestly, those bitches are usually right. I take a shower and do my hair and put on makeup before dressing in my cutest Christmas sweater. Bundling up in my coat and gloves and scarf and hat, I head out my front door and straight to the closest coffee shop, which is not the one I happen to work at.

It's cold outside, the kind that sinks into your bones, but it's dry at least, and I'm warm in my coat, and once I have a large peppermint mocha in my hands (apparently making approximately one thousand of them didn't fully kill their appeal), the warmth trickles through me from the inside out. I make my way over to the subway station and hop on a train to Manhattan. I love Brooklyn with my whole heart, but there's nothing quite like Christmas in Manhattan.

I start my holiday tour at the tree in Rockefeller Center. It's a classic for a reason, and this year's tree might be the most beautiful yet. I allow myself five whole minutes to think about all the times I came here with Nick, and surprisingly, the memories leave me with the warm and fuzzies instead of the usual cold and stabbies. I contemplate trying to rent some ice skates, but I want to enjoy my day, and that will be much harder with a broken ankle. When I've absorbed the full magic of the tree, I walk over to Bryant Park and stroll the winter market, stopping for some hot chocolate that's so rich it makes my blood sing in my veins. Honestly, the hot chocolate does more for my mental health than any wine and *Real Housewives* marathon could, and that's saying something.

After exploring the entirety of the winter market, I walk over to the Drama Book Shop. There's nothing particularly Christmassy about it, it's just one of my favorite places to be and that's what today is all about. I buy a new book and a croissant and sit for a bit before moving on to my next location, the Macy's on Thirty-Fourth Street. I mean, there's a whole classic holiday movie about it, so it's a must.

I don't actually go into the store because it's Christmas Eve and I don't have a death wish, but I do people-watch outside for a bit, loving how the holiday spirit makes even the surliest of New Yorkers smile.

I grab a late lunch of tomato soup and grilled cheese at a diner before deciding to pack it in and call it a day. Being out among the holiday joy has definitely helped bolster my spirits, but I know we're rapidly approaching the point when the afternoon shifts into evening, and the day becomes less about errands and more about spending time with family and friends.

So I head back to the subway and make my way home to my favorite borough. When I trudge up the stairs to my apartment, I'm surprised to find a box sitting on my welcome mat. Normally, packages are left downstairs near the mailboxes, and I don't think I'm expecting any orders, unless I did some dream shopping last night, which is always a possibility.

But the box doesn't have a mailing label. Instead it says, in bright-red letters: "To Jess, Love Santa."

Figuring my parents must have arranged this somehow, I bend over to pick up the box, but the thing is heavy, so I end up just nudging it inside with my foot instead. I bound into my tiny kitchen and grab a pair of scissors, cutting into the box like a kid on Christmas. Which I basically am.

It takes a minute to make sense of what I'm seeing in the box. There are six manuscripts piled inside, the kind publishers send out for early reads. They don't look like real books because the paper is regular letter size, but they're professionally bound.

I sit down next to the box, removing the first one and running my fingers over the title. It's *Heartbreak Manor*, Nick's first book. But why would he be sending me a weird version of his book? I already have the published version (in hardcover and paperback, if we're being honest). And this doesn't look old, the paper is crisp and fresh and smells like it came right off the printer.

I flip through the pages, wondering what I could even be looking for. The words of this book in particular are so familiar to me, I know them as well as I would my own. I must have read this manuscript a hundred times. I run my fingers over the words, and my chest starts to ache. I can practically hear his voice in my head, narrating to me as he wrote his favorite scene.

I keep flipping through the pages until I get to the end of the book.

My forehead wrinkles because something about the last two chapters feels off. Different. I know I've read these words before, but they somehow seem out of place.

My eyes widen as the full picture in front of me crystallizes. This isn't the end of the book that Nick published. It's the original ending, with his two characters reconciling their differences and ending up together. It's a happily ever after, the way a romance is supposed to end.

I set the first manuscript to the side and reach for the second. I read this one for the first time the day it was released, just like everyone else. Still, I've read it enough times to be familiar with the story, so I skip to the end. In the original version of this book, the heroine ends up leaving the hero to go marry the man her parents chose for her. It's absolutely devastating—I threw my book against the wall the first time I read it. But in this new version, she ditches her betrothed and runs away with the hero. They live happily ever after.

The next three books are the same. Nick has rewritten the endings of each of his published books so that the couple ends up together. No one dies, no one leaves, no one ends up alone and heartbroken. He's given all his characters happily ever afters, for me.

I don't stop to think about how he managed to do this, I'm too lost in the happiness, the joy that's emanating from these pages.

When I pull the final manuscript from the box, an excited squeal escapes me.

"*Just One Thing I Need* by Jessica Carrington and Nick Matthews" is inked on the cover.

I run my fingers over the title, and our names, relishing the tiny shiver of joy that darts through me to see them written together.

I hoist myself off the ground, take a bathroom break and get myself a snack and a beverage, because I know once I start reading this book—our book—I'm not going to want to stop.

Curling up in my favorite reading chair, the Christmas tree lights twinkling next to me, I cover myself with my softest blanket and open the book to read our story. I promise myself to read not as one of the authors, but as a reader experiencing it for the first time. I'm not going to worry about typos and plot holes, I'm going to focus on the journey of these characters we've created.

I spend the next couple of hours with a smile etched on my face. I think I might love this book, not something I can say about every first draft I've ever written, but this one, it has the sparkle. The it factor. We were able to find joy in writing it, and that joy is evident on the page.

What's also evident is the way Nick and I were able to seamlessly merge our voices, the way they complement each other, never competing or speaking over each other. It's like we were meant to be writing partners from the very beginning.

When I find myself reading a sex scene, one that Nick wrote on his own and that I haven't read yet, I bolt up straight in my chair. It's the spiciest thing Nick has written in a long time, and it heats my blood just reading the words on the page. And then my brain can't help but imagine me and Nick, and I have to take a short break to go pour myself a glass of wine.

The book is full of banter and wit, and yet my heart aches when the characters think they've blown their second chance. I know I'm the one who wrote the breakup, but I read it with fresh eyes and see how it's not really a breakup, more like a little pause. A chance for these characters to take a breath and really commit before they find their way back together.

And they do find their way back to each other because Nick has written the ending. A gorgeous grand gesture and a reconciliation and an epilogue that clearly proves our couple will live happily ever after.

I wipe the tears from my eyes and swig the last of my wine.

It's almost midnight, and I don't want to disturb him or wake him, but the need to talk to him outweighs anything else.

I hit his name in my contacts. I don't know what I'm going to say, mostly I just need to hear his voice.

"Hey, Jess."

"Hi."

There's a moment of awkward silence.

Okay, so we're not off to a brilliant start, but it's late.

"I got your package."

"Yeah?"

It speaks to the weight of the moment that neither of us makes the requisite *package* joke.

"I love you," I blurt out, unable to keep the words in any longer. If I'm being totally honest, I've been feeling them for longer than I would like to admit. If I'm being totally honest, I never stopped loving him in the first place.

"I love you too, Jess."

I release the breath I didn't realize I was holding, suddenly with a greater understanding for the characters I've been writing for so long. "I miss you, and I wish you were here. I wish we were going to be spending Christmas together."

"Well, you're in luck then."

There's a knock on my front door and since it's late and I live alone, my first instinct is to grab the baseball bat I keep in the hall closet.

But then I realize there's only one person who could be on the other side of that door.

I still check the peephole, just in case.

I open the door with a smile, ending our phone call and tossing my phone who cares where. "Hi."

"Hi."

A second later I'm in his arms, my face buried in his

neck, his grip on me so tight I almost lose my breath. But I only squeeze him back tighter.

He pushes the door closed behind him and lets me go, putting just enough space between us that he can take my face in his hands. "I'm so sorry, Jess. I was a total idiot, for a lot of things, but mostly for not just talking to you."

"I really wish you would have, but it happened and it brought us to where we are today. I'd much rather focus on the future."

"Me too." Nick leans in and presses a soft kiss to my forehead. "I want to focus on building something new with you, but I'll always regret the time we lost, that I let stupid career concerns cost me the love of my life."

"I assume you're referring to me?" I poke him in the stomach and grin.

"Obviously." He pulls me in closer. "I know I messed up, and I know a lot has happened in the five years we've been apart. But I never stopped loving you, Jess, and I never will. Do you think you can give me another chance?"

I let out a long, dramatic sigh. "That depends."

His eyes crinkle with worry. "On what?"

"Are you going to keep writing happily ever afters, or am I going to have to read a bunch of books where everyone dies in the end?"

He grins, and it lights up his eyes. "Okay, first of all, I have never written a book where everyone dies at the end. Second of all—"

I cut off his diatribe with a kiss, rising up on my toes to bring us even closer. He threads his hands through my hair and I open to him, fully and completely. Nick Matthews is the love of my life, the man who owns my heart—my fated mate—and I cannot wait to see what the next chapter brings.

We finally part, breathless, as church bells begin to toll across Brooklyn.

I grin. "I think that sound means it's officially Christmas."

Nick leans down for another kiss. "Best Christmas ever?"

"Best Christmas ever."

Epilogue

NICK

Next Christmas

For the past five years, when I've woken up on Christmas, it's felt like any other day. But today, I feel like, well, like a little kid waking up on Christmas.

Today is going to be the happiest day of my life, and this time, there is nothing that's going to stand in the way.

The past year with Jess has been undoubtedly the best year of my life. Two months ago, we released our cowritten second-chance holiday romance to rave reviews. SVP sent us on a press tour together that took us around the country and landed us on the *New York Times* Best Sellers list. Some of my readers were disappointed by the happy ending I wrote, but most of them have been excited to come along with me for the ride.

It's safe to say the romance community as a whole has fully embraced our real-life love story. We did the morning talk-show circuit and made more than one host cry with our true tale of a second chance at love. Both the critics and the readers have eaten the book up, and SVP is clamoring for us to do more. Even though we have loose plans to write a second book together, we're also working on our own individual projects, and I love that we get to do both.

But today isn't about our readers or the SVP publicity department or any other love story but ours.

I bring Jess a peppermint mocha in bed, still not used to the thrill of seeing her curled up under my sheets. She moved in over the summer and getting to see her whenever I want has been fantastic, for my libido anyway, though not for the word count on the new manuscript I'm supposed to be working on.

What can I say? I just can't get enough.

And neither can she.

She pulls me down on top of her the moment I set down our mugs of coffee, and it doesn't take long before I'm buried inside of her and she's calling out my name.

Luckily, I built some time into our schedule for the day for unexpected trysts.

"I hate to say this," I say as I dot kisses up the side of her neck, "but we really do need to get moving."

She groans, shoving me off of her. "This better be good, Nick Matthews."

"You know I will deliver nothing less than the best Christmas ever."

She hits me with a pillow. "I'll be the judge of that."

"Go get ready, and make sure you're dressed in your holiday best."

She climbs out of bed, still naked, and saunters into the bathroom, knowing exactly what she's doing.

I spend the time she's in the shower getting dressed,

tucking the little black box into the inside pocket of my jacket. I kept the original ring from all those years ago, but something about giving it to her just didn't feel right. So I bought a new one, for the fresh start she so graciously gave me.

I hope she loves it.

Alyssa and Kennedy assure me she will. So do her parents, who welcomed me back into their lives just as graciously as their daughter did. They'll be meeting us later for dinner, though Jess thinks they are on another one of their cruises. I can't wait to see her face when she sees them.

We spend the day doing all of her favorite things, watching the ice-skaters at Rockefeller Center and drinking hot chocolate from the Bryant Park winter market. We stop for a casual lunch at one of our favorite diners and grab her third peppermint mocha from a small café before getting on the subway to head to our next stop.

The Strand isn't usually open on Christmas, but I called in a few favors, and when I open the door to the empty shop and see the look of awe on Jess's face, well, it was worth it. We held the final stop on our book tour here, one of the many items on Jess's author bucket list she's been able to check off this year, along with finally quitting her coffee shop job. As of two weeks ago, she's now officially a full-time writer.

I lead her to the rare book room, where Hilary has orchestrated all the details. Lights are strung from the ceiling, and a huge Christmas tree sits in the center of the space, with one wrapped gift waiting underneath.

Jess looks at me with wide eyes. "What's all this?"

"It's your Christmas present, obviously." I poke her in the ribs because if I don't ease some of the tension roiling in my gut, I might throw up before I can pop the question. "Open it."

Jess walks slowly over to the tree, like she's expecting something to jump out and scare her. She unwraps the small rectangular package carefully when all I want her to do is rip into the paper. Removing the lid from the box, she peeks cautiously inside. Her brow furrows and she turns to me in confusion. "What is this?"

"It's the dedication page of my next book."

"But it says . . ." Those gorgeous brown eyes widen even more as I sink to my knee.

"It says, 'This book is dedicated to the love of my life, my partner, my everything. My wife.'" I pull the ring box from my jacket and open it.

Her mouth drops open and the piece of paper with the dedication falls from her fingers and flutters to the ground. "Are you serious right now?"

"Of course I'm serious. Jess, you have always been the only woman for me. I wasted a lot of time, and I don't want to waste a second more. Will you marry me?"

"Hell yes, I'll marry you! Are you freaking kidding me?!?" She throws herself into my arms, and since I'm still down on one knee, the movement topples both of us over to the side.

I cushion her head before it can hit the wood floor. Before I can say anything, her mouth is pressed to mine and I gladly lean into the kiss.

Eventually I have to pull away because I don't think my

rental contract covers us having sex on the floor of the rare books room. Unfortunately.

I hop up, pulling Jess up with me. She pats down my hair and I straighten her sweater. "I think we forgot an important step here." I hold up the ring.

She slips her hand into mine, and I slide the ring on her finger. "A perfect fit."

I brush my lips over her knuckles. "A perfect fit."

"I love you, Nick Matthews."

"I love you, Jessica Carrington." I tuck her hand into the crook of my elbow. "Now come on, we're not done with the holiday magic just yet."

She snort-laughs as she leans her head on my shoulder. "I think it's time to admit I've fully converted you. You love Christmas just as much as I do."

I press a kiss to the top of her head. "Not going to lie. It's growing on me."

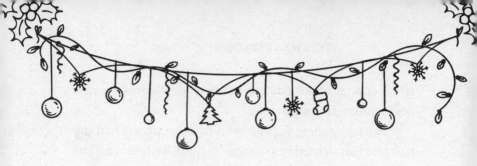

ACKNOWLEDGMENTS

Whew! What a whirlwind this book has been! Since this book is short and sweet, I'm going to try to keep these acknowledgments the same (lol)!

First and foremost, to my entire Putnam team. I feel so lucky to have landed somewhere where everyone has more faith in me than I often have in myself. I am so immensely grateful to everyone who had a hand in producing this book, but especially to my editor, Kate Dresser. Thank you, Kate, for taking what could have been a daunting and overwhelming few months and making the transition so unbelievably smooth.

Gaby Mongelli, this book is dedicated to you because, quite simply put, I wouldn't be here without you. Thank you for seeing something in me, and for helping me grow.

My agent, Kimberly Whalen, continues to be an absolute rockstar. Thank you for holding my hand and assuaging my fears, and being the best advocate for my career.

Courtney Kae, Corey Planer, Ashley Hooper, Brianna Mowry, I love you all.

To my romance writer community, I'm keeping this brief, so I won't name you all, but I could not survive this without you.

To my readers, you bring me such joy. There are no words for how much you mean to me, and how appreciative I am of your support.

To my family, thank you always.

To Canon, maybe one day I'll write a book you're actually allowed to read, but until then, thanks for being the best kid ever.

And to Matt, I couldn't do it without you. Like, for real. Love you the most.

Photo credit: Brianna Mowry

FALON BALLARD is the author of *Lease on Love*, *Just My Type*, and *Right on Cue*, and cohost of the podcast *Happy to Meet Cute*. When she's not writing fictional love stories, she's helping real-life couples celebrate, working as a wedding planner in Southern California.

Visit Falon Ballard Online

falonballard.com
FalonBallard
FalonBallard